Briarley

Aster Glenn Gray

BRIARLEY

CHAPTER 1

There once was a country parson with a game leg from the Somme, who lived in a honey-colored parsonage with his daughter, the most beautiful girl in the world.

Others might have quibbled that Rose was not the most beautiful girl in the world, or even the prettiest girl in the village of Lesser Innsley. But to the parson she was all loveliness, all the more so because his wife died when their Rose was still very young, and so Rose was all he had left to love in this world.

And for most of Rose's childhood, it was a world of peace if not plenty. She liked to sit and read in the window seat in the parson's study, which overlooked the garden. In the fall she would reach out the open window to pluck a pear from the tree espaliered to the parsonage wall; and the parson would say, absently, "Don't get juice on the books, Rose."

She did sometimes get juice on the books. But

she read them, too, book after book, and talked about them with him as they walked together in the garden in the evenings. They both loved detective fiction, and put on black armbands the day that Sir Arthur Conan Doyle died, which greatly confused Rose's teacher Miss Clarence when she came to tea that afternoon.

And so the years passed quietly. Rose left home to attend a women's college in Oxford. The parson was sorry to see her go, and missed her sorely, and yet was glad that she went to his own university, where he had passed happy years.

But then war came again.

Rose left Oxford to become a nurse. Her letters were as light and sparkling as ever, but the parson's heart was sore for her, for he knew what war hospitals were like.

One weekend in late summer, she received an unexpected leave. The parson did not know she was coming until she arrived, and he had already promised to go into the county town to discuss the removal of London's children to the countryside.

"Of course I must not interrupt your war work," Rose said, and she smiled.

But the parson saw how worn and sad she looked behind that smile. "I will bring you a rose," he told her. "As I used to do, when you were younger, and I had to go away."

For Rose, after her mother went away and died in hospital, used to become nearly inconsolable when her father's work called him away from home overnight: and so he had begun the custom of always bringing her a rose. These roses they pressed solemnly between the pages of a book, where they would retain their sweetness. "And if you miss me, Rose my child," the parson used to tell her, "open the book and smell the roses, and know that I will come back to you."

Older now, and knowing how many people go away and do not come back in times of war, Rose caught her breath, and her eyes misted. "Oh, Dad," she said; and she might have said more, but she looked up and saw the wistfulness in his face, and remembered that he had his own war, when he had been young. "Please, Dad," she said more gently. "Bring me a rose."

But the parson almost forgot. He did not know the county town well: it was farther from home than he usually went, and his wounded leg ached by the time he arrived. He sat in his meeting and rubbed his leg and reflected ruefully that he should not have ridden his bicycle so far. But what was done was done.

He gave his speech and had his tea and discussed the necessities of war in grave tones. The meeting dragged on, and on, and on, as meetings will. And the upshot of it all was that the parson forgot the rose until he was out of town. His leg hurt too much to turn back; but the thought of that forgotten rose grieved him more than he could say.

Perhaps grief clouded his eyes. Something must have: for on the way home, he took a wrong turning, and could not find his way back. The road signs had all been taken down, so the Germans would not be able to find their way around if they came to the shores of England. "And if they are as confused as I am," the parson complained, stopping in the gathering dusk beneath a great oak tree, "perhaps they will just turn around, and go back to France."

He turned around himself – although he had turned around before, and somehow only ended up more lost – and then he stopped, for in the turning he saw something that he had not seen before. There was a great iron gate, and beyond a long white drive lined by great tall hedges of roses, that ended in a great grey pile of a house.

The parson eyed the fine raked gravel drive with no little bit of disapproval. Now here was a house that had not given its young menservants to the war effort.

Still, beggars cannot be choosers. The black clouds boiled above the house, and the air smelled thick with rain. The parson had spent his time sleeping in the rain in the trenches in France: he would seek shelter from the storm at that great house. Quite likely they would be on the 'phone, and he could call Bert at the Green Man, who could send a message to Rose to tell her not to worry. Then the parson could spend the night here safe and dry, and even take a rose with him in the morning.

For the roses were magnificent. Even in the dimness of the stormy dusk the red petals shone bright. The parson, an amateur gardener himself, eyed them in fascination as he trundled his bicycle up the lane, and wondered how the gardeners achieved such a uniform perfection. They must have been very quick to remove any wilted rose.

A few drops of rain fell on his face as he wheeled

his bike to the grand staircase at the front of the house. Surely someone must have seen his approach. But the doors did not open, and no footman came down the sweeping staircase, and the house remained dark and silent. Stately letters carved out the name of the place above the door. This was Briarley Hall.

The parson shivered. The cold wind whipped around him and seemed to propel him up the steps, although his bad leg protested the exertion. Still, there was nothing else for it now: the first wave of rain pattered down on the white gravel, turning it grey with wet.

Still the parson hesitated over the dragon-shaped knocker, which gazed at him with red garnet eyes. "As if it is going to turn into Jacob Marley's head," he muttered to himself. The cold wind blew a sheet of rain beneath the overhang, and a few drops reached even up the steps to the parson, and the parson shuddered and reached to knock.

Then he jerked away. A spark had leapt between his hand and the knocker.

The dragon knocker seemed to gaze at him, mocking. The parson hesitated, hand still half-raised, until a gust of wind drove the rain sideways and spattered across his back. Then he lifted the heavy knocker and brought it down.

Even through the thick wood of the front door, the parson could hear the sound of that knock reverberate through the front hall. He stood, and waited, and listened; but he heard no voices, no footsteps. The door did not open, and no footman came out, and the house remained dark and silent.

Although it was summer, the parson began to shiver from the chill of the rain. He raised the knocker again and brought it down three times. He could hear their echoes overlapping inside the house.

Then the downpour began in earnest. The parson gave up on politeness, and pushed hard at the door. It opened with such silent swiftness that he nearly fell inside.

CHAPTER 2

"Good evening," the parson called. His voice sounded tentative, although perhaps any voice would have sounded so beneath that vast cavern of a roof. Truly this was a great house, grander even than the country home of Lord Ashton, the parson's grandest Oxford friend; and he stood for some moments dripping on the tile floor, and waiting for someone to come, if only to tell him to leave.

But no one came. Thunder rumbled, and a spattering of rain blew in through the open door, which prompted the parson to close it. "Good evening," he called again, and took a few furtive steps deeper into the hall, like a child sneaking into his father's study.

There *must* be someone here. The house had none of that musty smell of a place that had been shut up. The tiled floor and the mahogany banister on the grand staircase gleamed, as if they had been polished that very afternoon. But no one appeared: no footman or housemaid, no daughter of the house peeping through the rail of the staircase. The hall was dim and rather cold.

Perhaps an invalid lived here: an invalid with a very small staff (although a very industrious one, to keep the grand staircase in such trim). Perhaps they all lived at the back of the house, and had not heard the parson above the drum of the rain of the roof.

"I hope it is not a strain on your ration books to feed a hungry traveler," the parson said to the empty hall, pitching his voice louder in the hope that it might be heard from further off. There was a bench tucked in beside the staircase, and he limped to it, and sank onto it with as much relief as if it had been a silken Ottoman. He rubbed his knee, his shin, and waited.

But no one came. The rain pounded on the roof, and the light from the windows grew dimmer.

And then the parson seemed to smell the succulent scent of roast beef.

It could not be, of course. No one had roast beef these days – not even in a great house like this. Could one smell a mirage?

But mirage or not, the aroma drew the parson irresistibly down the corridor. The smell of roast beef grew stronger, and now he seemed to smell the rich savory scent of Yorkshire puddings, as well – and if the scents must all be delusion, still, he could not be deceived in the flickering glow of a fire spilling from a doorway ahead.

And where there was a fire, there must be some inhabitant. No one could afford to light a fire in an empty room in these days.

But the dining room was empty too. Yet the

servants must have just left. The table was set extravagantly *a la francaise*, with all the dishes on it, and a joint at either end of the table: a whole roast suckling pig at the head, and a roast beef at the foot, and heaping corner dishes of steaming rolls, and sliced carrots gleaming in their butter like copper coins. A tower of apples stood as the centerpiece. Clusters of tiny lustrous champagne grapes cascaded down its sides.

Even up at the Hall, he had not seen such a feast since before the war began. But there was no one here, and no sound of anyone in the house: no distant tinkle of piano or rattle of cookware (though in a house this grand, of course he would not hear that), no approaching footsteps as the party processed to their dinner, or the butler came to check on the meal one last time.

The chill feeling he had first felt at the door returned, and this time there was no wind on which to lay the blame. A fire crackled in the corner fireplace. The room was toasty warm.

The parson did not believe in magic, in fairies; he strove to break the country folks in his parish of the habit. But here: an empty house, a tempting table, a price to be paid by the unwary wanderer who ate even one of those tiny grapes.

A bitter ancestral fear rose within him. It had been months since he had eaten good roast beef, and yet he found himself backing away.

"I am afraid," the parson said, still striving to speak courteously, in case the air was not so empty as it seemed, "that I must take leave of this place. I hope I have caused no trouble; I am very sorry."

He walked as swiftly as he could back the way he had come. The hall seemed to stretch far longer this time, and the feeling of being watched prickled up and down his back.

But he reached the front hall unharmed, and found that the rain had gone, and the moon glowed through the fan-shaped window above the tall door.

Had so much time passed as all that?

"I think you for your hospitality," the parson told the empty air. "And good night."

His fingers trembled as he reached for the doorknob. But it turned easily under his hand, and the door swung silently open.

A soft beautiful mist rose off the white gravel in the moonlit dusk, and sent another superstitious prickle shivering down the parson's back. He had not always been a parson. He had read English at Oxford, in his younger days, and knew all the old strange stories of Beowulf and King Arthur; and had bought and read with Rose all the fairy tale books of Andrew Lang.

"A fine story this will be for Rose," he said – for the sound of his voice comforted him – as did the solid metal handlebars of his bicycle. The fairy folk, he recalled, do not like cold iron. "She may very well think I had made it all up," he murmured; for already it began to seem strange to him, as he walked away. "But nonetheless she will like it."

The mist rose high and thick, so that the front wheel seemed to disappear into the fog. The parson felt uneasy as he looked at it, and uneasier still when his gaze fell further and he saw that he could not see his own booted feet in that mist. He looked hastily away.

And that was his undoing: for his gaze fell upon the roses again.

It seemed a great pity not to fulfill his promise to his daughter, when there were so many roses here and no one to miss them.

The parson propped up his bicycle on the gravel lane, and stole across the grass to the rose hedges lining the drive. The moonlight only enriched their velvet colors. Even in the silvery light the petals glowed wine-red.

The parson cupped one red rose in his hand: a flower as vast as a peony, its petals soft as a baby's skin. His penknife was dull, and it took him some few minutes to saw through the thick thorny stem. His thumb caught and tore on one of the wicked thorns, dripping red blood onto the green grass below.

But at last the knife won through. The stem had been sliced jagged, but the rose remained unblemished. The parson lifted it to his nose and took a sniff, and frowned. It did not smell as sweet as he thought it should.

But nonetheless he put it tenderly in his buttonhole, and patted it, and turned back toward the path, where the mist shrouded his bicycle. Only one handlebar rose visible above the thick white gauze of fog.

But the moment the parson set foot on the path, the iron gates swung shut. They crashed together with a terrible clang, and the parson stood frozen in surprise and creeping horror.

One did not steal the fairies' flowers either, it

seemed. One should not bleed on fairy ground.

"Thief!" a great voice roared, and the parson whipped around, looking for the source of it. "Thief! Thief! *Thief!*"

And then the parson was covered in shame. Could he have stolen a flower, like a schoolboy scrumping apples? "I'm sorry," he said. "I wanted it for my daughter; and your roses are so perfect, I did not stop to think…"

"Your daughter!" the voice shouted, and all at once the parson saw its source. The voice came from overhead, from a flying contraption that looked as if someone had built an enormous mechanical bat.

The parson stepped back, and back again, and might have run – but his mist-hidden bicycle betrayed him. He collided with the bicycle, and man and bicycle fell down on the path together.

The great flying thing flapped down to the path. Its wings swirled up the mist and stirred the gravel, sending a wave of grit into the parson's face.

The thing landed upright on its own two feet, and folded its wings sleekly back against its frock coat. The parson thought wildly of spies, or secret testing facilities for strange new flying weapons: for it looked as though this man wore wings on his back, like Daedalus. His head had been made monstrous by – was that a gas mask?

But the moonlight fell full on the man's face, and the parson saw with horror and fascination that he wore no mask. Nor was his deformity of the sort that many of the parson's comrades had suffered in the last war. Mustard gas could eat noses, and eyes, and whole faces; but it could not elongate a face into a scaly dragonish snout.

Nor give a man wings. The creature had folded them as neatly as a bird might, with no mechanical stiffness about it.

The parson's fascination almost overcame his terror. "What *are* you?" he asked.

A roaring rush of flame blew from the creature's snout. The flames did not reach the parson, but the heat blasted against him like a force, and parched his throat and scorched his cheeks, and pinned him to the ground.

The dragon-man leaped forward, wings flashing out so that they blocked the sky. He gathered the parson up in his arms and bore him into the air.

CHAPTER 3

They alighted on the roof of the mansion. The dragon set the parson down on the slick wet tiles, and the parson slipped, and for a sickening moment thought he might slip right off the roof and fall to his death – but he caught himself, and sat down hard.

The dragon stood above him, his spread wings a great black blot against the moonlit sky. Then he folded his wings, and with that he looked like a man again: a man powerfully built, broad-shouldered and strong-armed, but a man nonetheless.

The parson's terror ebbed. He rose to his feet, shakily, his leg throbbing, but determined at least that he would die standing up if it came to it.

"I'm sorry I cut your rose," the parson said. "I will pay for it, if you desire. But please, sir, let me go home to my daughter."

The dragon snorted. Little curls of flame licked out of his nostrils. "What do I need with a few shillings?" he asked, and gestured at the extent of

14

his lands. The rose garden seemed to have grown, so it stretched away into the distance, and the closed iron gate looked only a toy at the end of the long white drive.

"What need have you of a single rose? You have a sea of them," the parson countered.

Another snort, another flicker of flames. The fire briefly illuminated that dragon's dark eyes, and the parson saw that they were not slit-pupiled snake eyes, not beast eyes of any kind, but the eyes of a man.

"Do you think you are some Robin Hood of roses?" the dragon-man demanded. "I propose a trade."

"Oh?"

"Do you agree?" the dragon demanded. There was a hint of a growl beneath his voice.

"I can hardly agree without knowing the terms," the parson said sharply.

"Very well. You were taking the rose to your daughter, you say?"

The parson wished abruptly that he had not mentioned Rose.

He made no response, but the dragon did not seem to need one. After a slight pause, he continued, "I will free you if you will send her to me to take your place."

"Impossible." The parson's voice was flat.

The dragon stepped back. His claws clicked on the slate roof. "But it is very possible," he objected. "And she will be happy here, I promise. Here she can have all the roses she could ever want."

The parson almost laughed, it was so absurd. "I

do not think roses are all there is to happiness," he said.

"But she will have everything else as well," the dragon objected. "Plenty of food, and servants, and beautiful gowns. That is everything a woman could want. Is it not?"

"There is an old story," the parson said, "from the tales of King Arthur, which perhaps you know – the tale of Gawain and the Loathly Lady – "

The dragon snorted. Twin balls of flame rose from his nostrils. "Skip to the moral, parson," he said. "I hate parables."

"Then I shall cut to the chase, and tell you that a woman's own way is what she wants. And all the roses in the world will not make up for the lack of it," the parson said.

The dragon stamped one clawed foot so hard it broke a roof tile. "I could fling you off this roof," he said. "Do you want to die here?"

"No," the parson said. "But I did not want to die in a trench during the war either, and yet I would have done it if it came to that."

There was another pause. Flames flickered up from the dragon's snout again, lighting unholy sparks in his brown human eyes. "But that's different," he said. "You had no other choice then."

"Nor do I now," the parson said.

The dragon ground his teeth. "See reason!" he roared, and then calmed himself with an effort. "Come now, man. Send for your daughter and you can go free."

"I am being quite reasonable," the parson replied. "I will not buy my freedom at that price."

The dragon gave a furious scream that came out accompanied by a gout of flame. The fire fountained into the sky, and the dragon's wings unfurled, and flapped so powerfully that they knocked the parson off his feet again. He had to scramble at the tiles so as not to slip right off. By the time that he was steady again, the dragon was far distant, flying away like some great horrible bat.

"They'll have the Civil Defence after you," the parson called, although doubtless the dragon was too far away to hear. "You might as well put up a signal flare for the Nazis." He envisioned Luftwaffe pilots running into the dragon in the sky, and despite everything cracked a smile. "If the Luftwaffe gets you, it will be the only good work they ever did," he called after the dragon, although the dragon had already disappeared into the gloom.

A chill thin rain began to fall again. The parson sat up painfully. Summer it might be, but with the weather like this he might die of exposure up here, or at least take a great chill. He must get off this roof.

In his younger days, the parson and his dear friend Rupert Spiles had liked to climb the buildings at Oxford at night, so that they could be alone together in the darkness. But climbing down this hideous pile was quite out of the question, with his leg the way it was – and in any case, a smooth Palladian monstrosity like this would have few footholds. "Next time," the parson commented, and his teeth were beginning to chatter, "next time I shall arrange to be kidnapped by a dragon with the good taste to have a gothic mansion."

A flash of lightning forked across the sky, and illumined the roof for a precious second – and then the parson saw the dormer window, reflecting the lightning with dazzling brightness.

A *window*.

He was saved.

It was a long and weary passage across the roof to the window. Many and many a time he felt himself slipping, and clutched at the slick tiles with his numb fingers, and his hands were scraped and nicked and cut by the time he reached the window. He had ceased to shiver: he no longer felt the cold.

He rapped one battered knuckle against the windowpane. There was no answer.

The parson kicked his thick-soled boot through a pane of glass. He reached through and unlatched the window, and tumbled into the room.

The floor was satin-smooth, as well-polished as the floors below. There was no mustiness here, none of that neglected odor that little-used rooms took on: no smell of mice or cobwebs.

A very tidy-minded dragon he must be, to keep the whole place so clean. "He must," the parson said, and began to laugh in the wild way of someone far too tired, "he must have kidnapped an army of servants."

The parson dragged himself away from the window, out of the spitting rain. He knew, with some far distant part of his mind, that he ought keep moving. The dragon would come back to his house, surely, and could find that broken window, and find him again. But he was utterly spent, and the rain drummed on the roof; and the parson fell asleep.

CHAPTER 4

Now nothing in an English country village can ever remain a secret for long, certainly not the disappearance of its parson; and the news spread through Lesser Innsley on the very evening of his disappearance. His daughter Rose waited up for him, reading in an old favorite armchair before the fire as the rain beat softly on the roof, and trying not to worry. Surely her father had simply sought shelter from the rain in a pub, and had not thought to call.

But then the rain stopped, and he did not come. Rose read on, and he did not come; and she finished another chapter, and he did not come; and then she found herself sitting with the book closed over her thumb, gazing fixedly toward the fire, although she was not seeing it.

The clock began to strike. Rose sprang from her chair, as though the clock had released her just as it released its clockwork cuckoo; and she put on her mackintosh and galoshes and was shutting the door behind her before the final strike tolled.

The rain had passed, but puddles dotted the roads. Rose strode onward regardless, and the hem of her skirt was soaked by the time she reached the Green Man.

It was not common for a young girl to come to the Green Man so late on her own, and they all looked at her askance – but Rose, in the throes of her worry, didn't notice. "Bert," she said to the bartender. "Did my father call?"

At once Bert was all concern. "No, Miss Harper, he hasn't," he said. "Hasn't he come home?"

Rose shook her head. "I'm concerned…" she began, and trailed off.

"Perhaps the storm took the 'phone lines down," Bert suggested.

"Or the Hun," one of the men threw in, and fell silent when all the others frowned at him.

"It was a bad storm, Miss," Jem Thatcher said. "Even the Germans wouldn't be out in it, I don't doubt."

"It's not the Germans I'm worried about," Rose said. "It's his leg. He took his bicycle, you see, all the way to the county town, and I'm afraid that he… that he might have gotten tired," she finished lamely, although that was the least of her fears. She feared a crash, or a collapse; she feared he might be lying sodden in the road somewhere, unable to get to his feet.

"Don't you fret, Miss," Bert said. "Just as likely he stopped at a farmhouse that isn't on the 'phone." He paused, his bristly chin on his hand, and thought; and said apologetically, "It's just we can't go waving lights around, Miss. We'd be out looking for him else, but we don't want to signal the Luftwaffe, now. Your father wouldn't want that."

"Still and all," Jem Thatcher said. "There's enough of a moon we could look about, couldn't we? Just about the town, in case he's near home."

Look they did, that night. The next day, too, they looked, and contacted the villages around so they would look too. By the end of the day it seemed all the roads between the village and the county town had been searched, and no sign of the parson or his bicycle had been found.

And Rose's leave was at an end: she must catch the last train back. She sat on the station platform, her face very pale and her back very straight, both hands clasped about the handle of a battered old carpetbag that had been her mother's, long ago.

The village schoolmistress, Miss Clarence, sat beside her, and they did not speak till they knew the train was coming. It showed no headlight, but they could feel its rumbling approach long before they heard the wheels clacking on the tracks.

"Your father would want you to go," Miss Clarence said. She had been Rose's teacher, when Rose was a little girl, and she thought as she looked at her that she had not seen the child look so bedraggled and woebegone since her return to school after her mother's death. A laughing child had been replaced by a silent elf, just as a bright young woman now had been replaced by a statue. "He was very proud of you for joining up."

Rose drew in a deep breath – it might have been the first breath she had taken since they'd come to the station, for all Miss Clarence had seen – and stood, with the abruptness of a marionette pulled to its feet.

But her face softened as she turned to Miss Clarence. "You will contact me – the minute you find anything," she said, half an order and half a plea. "You will not try to spare me?"

Miss Clarence managed to wrest one of Rose's hands from the handle of the carpetbag, and held it in both her own. "We will not spare you," she said. "I will send the telegram myself, the moment that we have word."

The train puffed into the station. Blackout curtains covered its windows, and it was startling when the conductor opened the door, and light spilled out of that seemingly dark train car.

The light silhouetted Rose for a moment, as she gave the conductor her ticket. Then the door closed and the train pulled out of the station. It merged into the murky dusk. The rattle of its wheels on the rails faded and was replaced by the evening birdsong; and at last, even the rumble of the train's passing faded from the ground, and the train was gone.

CHAPTER 5

When the parson awoke, he was warm.

He was warm and enveloped in softness, and when he opened his eyes he found that it was morning, and the sunlight streamed in through a tall bay window, and lay in soft squares over the counterpane on the four-post bed where he lay.

He lay very still and tried to remember where he was and how he had gotten there, and could not; and in a frenzy of worry he threw back the covers and stood up.

His head swam and his bad leg nearly gave out, but he caught the bedpost and held himself up. His vision cleared, and he could see through the window, which showed an endless vista of tall blossoming hedges of roses, and a thin white gravel lane unspooling to a far distant black gate.

He sat down on the bed. The draft nipped at his legs, and he looked down and saw that someone had dressed him in an old-fashioned nightshirt, like an illustration out of Dickens.

He was in the dragon's lair still, then. And someone had brought him down to this room, and changed him out of his wet clothes. The parson could not imagine the dragon doing it. Did he have servants after all? A phalanx of kidnapped girls, perhaps.

Just then, a firm knock sounded on the door.

The parson's heart jumped. "Hello?" he called, hope rising in his breast. Perhaps this was a servant, after all. Perhaps at last all would be explained.

But the door did not open, and instead the servant spoke through it, her voice muffled by the thick wood. "The master wishes to see you for breakfast," she said.

"Who is your master?" the parson asked. "What is his name? Can you tell me where I am?"

"Your clothes are on the chair," the voice said. And then there was a rustle of cloth, and retreating footsteps. The parson struck a frustrated fist against the mattress.

Well, there was nothing for it but to breakfast with the dragon – and hope that the dragon did not intend him for the main course.

His clothes were clean and dry and pressed. The parson put them on and went to his door, which opened smoothly, and looked up and down the long hall – and realized he had no idea which way to go. His leg still ached, and he did not relish the idea of searching all over the house for the dining room; but still less did he want to miss the chance to reason with the dragon.

And, when he looked down the hall again, he saw that to the right, the candles were lit in sconces spaced along the wall. They had not been lit before, he thought.

He shook his head and stumped off down the hall, following the candles as one might follow a will-o-the-wisp through a swamp. He hoped they led him to a better end than will-o-the-wisps were wont to do.

The candles led him down a spiral stair and a wide hall. He was weak still, and the walking tired him so much that he could not even worry about his meeting with the dragon; and he was relieved when he came at last to a dining room. It was smaller than the cavern he had seen on his first night in this place, with the meal set in chafing dishes on a sideboard along the wall, and the table set for two, with a cushioned chair to one side and a stool to the other.

The parson snorted. The dragon meant to put him in his place, it seemed.

The dragon turned – and it was only then that the parson saw him, for he had been standing in the shadows by the bright window.

"Good morning," the dragon said, stepping forward so that the light shone on his face. He was attempting a smile, the parson thought, but the expression looked odd on his reptilian snout.

The parson did not smile back. The dragon hooked his taloned thumbs in the pockets of his brocade waistcoat. "My retainers tell me I have approached this poorly," he said.

"A kidnapping is generally a poor approach," the parson agreed.

The attempted smile snapped off the dragon's

face. His teeth clicked together and the scaly frill around his neck lifted. Then it smoothed again, as if from force of will, and that strange smile returned. "You will understand once I explain," he said, and gestured at the chafing dishes with one clawed hand. "But first, let's eat. You must be very hungry."

It was no use to argue with the gentry, and indeed, the parson found himself ravenous at the smell of the food. It was an English breakfast such as he had not seen since the war began: bacon and kippers, grilled tomatoes, thick slices of ham and thicker slices of toast, and all the butter anyone might desire. No rationing, it seemed, in fairyland.

This thought arrested the parson even as he took up a china plate. "You will excuse me," he said. "But this is not fairy food? I will not leave this place and discover that four and twenty years have passed overnight if I eat?"

The dragon had already filled his plate and sat down – on the stool; and the parson saw that it was meant to accommodate his wings. It was hard to read that reptilian face, but the dragon's shoulders drew up as if startled. "No," the dragon said. "That is no part of the enchantment on this place."

So the parson piled up his plate and took the chair. The toast crunched between his teeth, the taste of butter filling his mouth, and after weary months of margarine he nearly cried at the taste.

"But," said the dragon. There was a suppressed eagerness in his voice. "You are right to suspect magic here. I am under a curse."

"A curse?" said the parson, and tried to suppress

his own eagerness: here at last, an explanation.

The dragon nodded. He had piled his plate with kippers, and swallowed them whole, without chewing, tipping his head back so they went down his throat – and the parson wondered how often he ate; if, like a snake, he might have one meal in a month, and rest sated on that, or if he still needed to eat as much as any warm-blooded creature.

The dragon ate three kippers, swallowing slowly, and the parson thought he was savoring the suspense. This impression grew stronger when the dragon washed his fish down with a mouthful of tea, which he drank from elegant Spode china, with one claw hooked through the handle.

"Nearly a hundred years ago," he said, "an enchantress came here in disguise, and after I had turned her out, she laid a curse on me and all my house. I must learn to love, she said, and be loved in return, or else the curse would hold us all forever." He gazed intently at the parson. "The enchantress's deadline is nearing. If I don't break the curse, I and all my people will be trapped like this – forever. So you see why I must have your daughter."

The parson was not edified. "You're going about this all wrong," he said. He spoke with some asperity – more than he would have allowed himself if he were speaking to one of his parishioners; but then none of his parishioners had ever kidnapped him. "That's not how you learn to love, not at all. Love is patient, love is kind. It does not envy, it does not boast, it is not proud. It does not dishonor others, it does not kidnap – "

"You're misquoting," the dragon interrupted.

"Paul doesn't say anything about kidnapping."

"So you do know your First Corinthians, after all," the parson said. The dragon glared, and the parson gripped the table, and went on. "I am paraphrasing. I believe the injunction against kidnapping is implied by all the rest of it."

"If you know your Bible so well," the dragon said, "then you know the Bible tells you not to steal."

"I apologize," the parson said steadily. "I have told you I will pay you for the flower."

"And I have told you the payment I desire!" the dragon roared.

"Then we are at an impasse," said the parson, "for my daughter is not mine to offer."

The dragon mused. "She is engaged?"

"She is very much engaged," the parson said gravely, for it was true, in its way: Rose was very much engaged in war work, in her studies, in a great many things that did not involve catering to the moods of a dragon.

The dragon slumped back in his seat and pressed his hands over his eyes. Those hands still looked quite human – except that they were tipped in claws. "I'm doomed," he said.

The attitude was so like something from a poor melodrama that the parson would have laughed, had his memory of the dragon's fiery outbursts not restrained him. Instead he ate his breakfast (and was glad to discover that it had gone cold, like normal food, rather than remaining ever-hot), and waited for the dragon to lift his head.

The dragon did not. The parson felt an unwilling

flicker of pity. "Come now," he said. "It's not so bad as all that."

"It is," the dragon said. His voice had the muffled broken sound of someone speaking through tears. "I have a hundred years to break the curse; and those hundred years will end in October."

"Well," said the parson, "you've simply been going at it all wrong, that's all. The curse says you must learn to love and be loved, does it not? Those are the only conditions?"

The dragon nodded, his head still buried in his hands.

The parson broke a piece off a roll and buttered it. "Then I suggest you get a puppy," he said.

The dragon jerked his head upright again. "A puppy!" he snarled, indignant. "The curse says nothing about a puppy."

"It says nothing about a maiden either," the parson rejoined. "I see no reason not to give a puppy a try. If you feed it and play with it, it will love you within a week, and puppies are very easy to love in return, I find. I have seen men broken by war put together again by a good dog." Indeed the parson's reunion with his own Irish setter had been a great help to him after he had returned home wounded from the Somme. "They can bring people who are nearly dead of sorrow back to life."

The dragon gazed at him. Despite all his years of experience at reading faces, the parson found it hard to read the expression on the dragon's snout. Disdain, perhaps, or horror. Certainly he was not pleased.

The parson's heart thumped. He broke off

another piece of his roll and buttered it too, with his best appearance of nonchalance. "At very least, a puppy will give you something to do other than mope."

The dragon bristled – not in the metaphorical sense that a human might bristle, but a true bristling of the scaly frill along his neck. "I do not sit around and mope all day," he said indignantly.

"Forgive me," the parson said mildly. "Is it you, then, who keeps the house and grounds in such spotless order, and cooks these delicious meals?"

The dragon snorted. "I have servants for that," he said, his mouth curving with disdain.

"Girls you've kidnapped?"

"*No,*" said the dragon. He sounded wounded. "Is that what you think of me?"

"Of course," the parson responded.

The dragon tried to reply, and couldn't, and clicked his teeth together and went back to his kippers.

"I haven't seen the servants," the parson added.

"You wouldn't. They keep out of sight to outsiders," the dragon said.

"Are they dragons like you?" the parson asked.

The dragon snorted. "They are not at all like me."

And he would not be drawn out further on the subject. The parson did not try too hard. He felt tired again, like a clockwork toy winding down, and he wanted to rest.

He was not sure how to take his leave – if he ought to ask to be excused, or clear his dishes. At length he said, "I find I am still weak from my recent indisposition. I hope you do not mind if I go away to rest."

The dragon waved a clawed hand. He was scowling at his kippers, his vast shoulders hunched in, and his whole attitude still so redolent of misery that it was almost funny.

And yet it touched the parson too, and rather against his will, he stayed at the table a little longer. "What is your name?" he asked.

The dragon lifted his head. "The servants call me master," he said. "The girls have called me beast."

"The girls?" the parson said sharply.

"They left," the dragon said. "None of them could love me." He drew in a deep breath and let it out slowly. "You ought to go too," he said. "You were my final hope, but you are useless to me."

The parson's heart thumped with hope and fear. Of course he would like to go home: but if the dragon turned him out of doors right now, he did not think he would make it out the estate's gate. "If you would lend me the use of your carriage," the parson said, "and take me to the nearest town, I would be glad to leave you in peace."

The dragon shook his head. "Unless driverless carriages have become common," he said, "as I hear horseless carriages have – no. It is impossible."

"Then I am afraid I must stop here until I am recovered."

The dragon's jaw clenched. He growled, and the sound was the more frightening because the parson did not think it was conscious. "Do as you will," the dragon snarled, and he left, his wings trailing behind him like a black opera cloak.

The parson sat a little longer, waiting for his strength to return. It occurred to him that if he waited long enough, one of the servants must surely come to clear away the breakfast, and that might be another mystery solved.

And perhaps one did. But his exhaustion got the better of him before it happened, and he fell asleep with his head pillowed on his arms on the shining table, and woke to find that someone had slipped a pillow beneath his arms and a blanket round his shoulders, so gently that he had not stirred at the touch.

CHAPTER 6

This little mystery of the pillow and the blanket offered a pleasant distraction from the more vexing question of the curse. The parson could not imagine that the dragon had a hand in it (or, as it were, a claw): that would require a thoughtfulness that seemed quite alien to him.

It must be the servants, then. And it must have been those unseen kindly servants who had found him in the old servant's bedroom, and brought him downstairs into the warmth, and probably saved him from pneumonia.

He must thank them. And, more, he must speak to them: servants always knew everything, and could doubtless shed more light on the question of this curse.

"I don't suppose," he said, "that you are somewhere about, you servants? I wish very much to thank you."

The parson listened, hopeful, but of course there was only silence. He sighed.

He might simply wait until the servants came to find him again. But he did not feel like waiting, and in any case, there was no need: one could always find servants in the kitchen of a great house.

Long before the parson found the kitchen, he could hear and smell it: the clang of pans, the wet scent of boiling water, the shrieking delighted laugh of a girl. As the parson got closer, he could hear the words too, and paused in the hallway in case he might overhear something important in eavesdropping.

But they were discussing neither himself nor their curse, but arguing with laughing high spirits. "There's no call to eat them all up, my girl," a woman said tartly.

"Oh, but there is! They're so good!" a girl cried in response, and the parson recognized the voice of the girl who had knocked on her door that morning. There was a sound like a smack, and the parson envisioned a cook swatting a young girl's hand as she reached for some delectable sweet.

So vivid was the imagining that it seemed very odd indeed to come to the door and see no one, although a tiny gooseberry tart hovered in midair. It remained there, frozen, in the sudden silence that greeted the parson's arrival; and then moved sideways suddenly, as if grabbed (a swiftly muffled exclamation supported the parson in this supposition) and became half a gooseberry tart, and then disappeared entirely.

And then the room was silent. A pan boiled over on the stove, and smoke billowed up, and when no one saved it the parson limped toward it, and twisted a dishtowel round his hand to remove it from the heat. "You needn't hush on my account," the parson said mildly. "I know you're here. This invisibility – it's part of the curse your master mentioned, isn't it?"

A few excruciating moments of absolute silence passed. The parson pulled out a chair at the rough kitchen table, mostly because his leg ached. But perhaps the sense that he felt easy enough to sit had some effect on the servants: for after he sat, there was a sound like an exhalation, and then a woman's voice said, "So the master did tell you about that. We told him he ought. It makes everything easier."

The parson inclined his head in the direction of the voice, which seemed to come from beside the stove. "You are the ones who brought me down to the bedroom, are you not? I must thank you."

"We could hardly leave you up there like a wet cat." This was a deeper voice, masculine. "I've learned my lesson, if Mr. Briarley hasn't."

"We've had an easier lesson to learn, maybe," the woman replied.

"There's nothing so hard about learning not to leave your guests to drown in the rain," said the girl.

The parson cleared his throat. "If I may ask, to whom do I have the honor of speaking?"

"Mrs. Price," the woman's voice said. "I'm the cook. And we've got Annie here, as was the dairy maid."

A bundle of carrots rose off the table and waved cheerfully at the parson. "It's good to see you looking so well," the girl's voice said.

"I'm pleased to meet you," he said, gazing at

some point left of the carrots, in the hopes that it was Annie's face. He did not think it was successful; she laughed, not unkindly.

"Don't go laughing at the quality, Annie," Mrs. Price said.

"Yes ma'am," said Annie, not much abashed; and she went on at once, "And Hugh's here too, who was the second footman."

"How do you do?" said the deeper voice, and the parson, who could not tell whence it come, bowed gravely to the room.

"I am well enough," the parson said, "thanks to your care. But full of questions about this place, as you might imagine, and I did not want to awaken painful memories in your master by asking them. Although perhaps it is painful to you too; it seems very hard for you to be cursed when it was your master who turned the enchantress away."

"Oh no, sir," Mrs. Price said. The parson thought this was the politeness of a servant who wished to keep her place, putting a good face on it before the gentry; but she went on, "We all turned her out too, see. She stopped by the dairy first, to ask Annie for a bit of whey; and when Annie said her nay, she come to the kitchen to beg a bit of a bread and a warm corner by the stove to sleep in, only I shut the door in her face. Too busy with preparations for the ball to have pity on one of God's creatures. It's like the tale of Sodom and Gomorrah, it is," Mrs. Price said, almost dreamily. "The Lord promised to spare the city if Abraham could find ten good men in it, but he couldn't; no more than the angel could find a single good soul among us."

"The enchantress, Mrs. Price," Annie said. "I don't think angels go about laying curses on people."

"Well, and who thought enchantresses walked the earth either, in this day and age?" Mrs. Price demanded. "One's as likely as the other, isn't it?"

"I was the last to see her," Hugh said, gently interrupting an argument that sounded as though it had been rehearsed many times in the last century. "The master asked me to throw her out the gate, after she disrupted his birthday ball. She came right in through the front door, like she was quality herself, when she was just a ragged old hag. Anyone would've thrown her out."

Mrs. Price snorted.

"Well, they would've," Hugh said stubbornly. "He laughed at her and told me to throw her out, and she shouted that curse as I was dragging her out of the room. 'You'll pay for this," she said. "A hundred-years curse upon you,' she said. 'You'll learn to love and be loved, or you'll be as ugly as your own heart – forever.' I had a bit of bread in my pocket," he added. "Maybe if I'd given it to her, we might have been spared all this."

"Don't be silly," Mrs. Price said. "Maybe she'd have spared you, but the rest of us were doomed by then, no doubt. The bells were practically tolling midnight when you put her out of the gate."

"The bells?" the parson asked. He had heard no bells in this place.

"The church bells, which haven't been heard here since, on account of it's a cursed place and God's turned his back," Mrs. Price said dolefully.

"He never," Annie said stoutly. "I don't think God turns his back on anywhere anymore, Mrs. Price. That was his promise to Noah with the rainbow."

"And when's the last time you saw a rainbow round here?" Mrs. Price demanded.

"Anyhow," said Hugh – the hastiness in his voice suggested he was interrupting another long-standing argument – "The curse came down at dawn the next day. The last carriages had just left, and most of us servants gone to bed, and then I heard the master shout. And when I went up to him, I found him just how he is now."

"Looking like Satan that's in the church window at Briarfield," Mrs. Price put in.

"And the lot of us invisible," Hugh said. "And that's how we've been ever since."

A dreary little silence followed. At last the parson broke it. "Are the three of you running this big place on your own?"

"No, love," Mrs. Price said. "The house runs itself, mostly. Keeps itself clean, and weeds the garden, and lays out a feast every night, just like how it was that last day."

"Made your breakfast, too, which it doesn't usually," Annie added.

"Perhaps the house is just as tired of all this as we are," Hugh said. His voice sounded heavy. "How long do we have left? The curse was laid All Hallow's Eve in 1840."

"It is August 1940," the parson said.

A china cup fell and shattered. "It can't be a hundred years already!" Annie cried.

"Annie!" Mrs. Price scolded.

"Well, and we've tried so hard! And it's all for naught, and the devil will climb out of the grate in the garden and drag us all to Hell!" Annie cried. "And all on account of you wouldn't send for you daughter – "

The parson had no time to formulate a reply before Mrs. Price rounded on Annie. "Oh, as if any of the other girls have done any good!" Mrs. Price cried. "The master's too sunk in his misery to notice Mary Magdalene if she came up and offered herself to him, and that's a fact."

"There have been other girls?" the parson said. Anything to lead the conversation away from Rose.

"Sure and we've tried," Mrs. Price said. "First thing we did was send out invitations to all the old county folk who used to visit."

"And the master hid away in the dungeons and wouldn't see anyone," Annie said. Her voice sounded choked with tears. "If he'd let Miss Pryor see him, she might have cried on him and smoothed back his hair and we all would've been saved, simple as that, but *no*! Oh, not him!"

"And is it your place to criticize the master, Annie?" Mrs. Price asked.

"It can't be criticism to state the plain facts," Annie insisted.

"Anyhow," Hugh interceded, "none of them stayed long, though we laid out a lovely collation and all. Certainly no one went searching down the dungeons. And he'd just have gone out the back way if they had."

"Once we'd given up on them, I sent out

advertisements for a governess," Annie said. "I got the idea out of *Jane Eyre*."

"But mostly the girls left after a few days," Mrs. Price said. "Smelled a rat, they did, and who could blame them? Rattling around this big empty house like peas, and no sign of a child to look after."

"So he wasn't threatening to throw people off the roof then?" the parson asked drily.

"*Did* he?" said Mrs. Price. She sounded appalled, and there was a long pause, and then she said hurriedly, "It's only 'cause the end's so near, love. I suppose the master's getting desperate. If he'd met more of the girls earlier..." Then she stopped: realizing, perhaps, that this was veering perilously close to criticism. "He couldn't bear to be seen," she said, as if in excuse. "Even by us, even for years."

"He was that vain before the transformation," Annie told the parson. "He had the loveliest gold hair, like a girl's, and beautiful broad shoulders – and it all turned against him after. He used to go through the house and break all the mirrors, only by morning they was always good as new, and he couldn't bear anyone to look at him, wouldn't even see most of the girls we brought. Oh!" She choked, and then cried out: "He could've broken the curse years ago! We're all doomed as doomed on account of him!"

"Annie!" Mrs. Price said sharply.

"Oh, you *won't* box my ears!" Annie cried. A stool fell over. Something knocked against the parson; and behind him, a door opened and then slammed. Annie had run out of the kitchen.

Another long silence followed. The door opened and closed again, very softly, and the parson thought Annie must have come back; but she did not speak, and then the parson thought that perhaps Hugh had gone after her.

The kettle whistled. It rose into the air, and steaming streams of water poured into two solid teacups. The kettle clanged on the stovetop again, and Mrs. Price said, "Even if you had a hundred daughters you was willing to send us, I don't see as it would help. The master's so set in his ways, I don't see how he *can* learn to love when he's left it this late. He's failed again and again, bless his soul. You may as well get out while you can."

"Oh," said the parson – and found, with great surprise, that he did not want to go. "It seems to me," he said slowly, "that I have been called here to help you."

"Suit yourself," said Mrs. Price, not unkindly. One of the teacups rose in the air, and crossed the room to him, and he felt the brief swish of her skirts against his trouser leg – which was an odd thing to feel indeed, when there was no one to see. "You can't make things any worse, bless you. Only you'd best leave before the curse ends."

"Do you know what will happen then?" the parson asked. "Did she say?"

"She didn't as such," Mrs. Price said, and she let out a quiet sigh. An oven door opened, and a pan of scones floated out, and settled gently on a counter. "But she said our hearts are stone; and it's my belief we'll turn into stone all over, when the time is up. Or perhaps pillars of salt."

41

The second teacup, which still sat on the counter, rose from its place. It tilted, and the liquid seemed to rise and crest above the lip of the cup, so it should have fallen; but it must have gone into Mrs. Price's invisible mouth. She set down the steaming cup. "I wonder," she murmured, "if we'll be visible then."

CHAPTER 7

The dragon summoned the parson to breakfast the next morning – or at least Annie said he had; the parson had some suspicion that the girl had badgered him into it.

Certainly he did not pay the parson the least attention as they ate breakfast together, but swallowed kipper after kipper with an abstracted expression. It reminded the parson rather of the breakfasts of his childhood, when his father sat with his newspaper raised like a shield between himself and his children.

The parson rather suspected that his father could not have managed enough love to disenchant his modest terrace house, had it ever fallen under a spell – and he certainly wouldn't have had any truck with beggar women bursting into birthday dinners, so perhaps it was only luck that saved him.

"Do you take the newspaper?" the parson asked.

"A newspaper?" The dragon blinked at the parson as if he had forgotten he was there. "Why should we? We are utterly cut off from the world."

"Not utterly," the parson objected. "I got in. The war itself may come to you, in the end."

"The war?" the dragon said: and the parson realized, boggling, that they did not yet know of the war here. "Are the French poised to invade?"

"The French!" the parson cried; and then recalled that, in 1840, when the house had been caught in time like a fly in amber, the most recent war would have been the Napoleonic.

"No," the parson said. "With Germany. We hope there won't be a land invasion, but they have been dropping bombs from aeroplanes."

A long silence followed this explanation: and the parson realized it must be a great deal for a man from 1840 to take in. "The Prussians conquered the rest of the German states," the parson explained. "And now they are trying to conquer the rest of Europe."

"By dropping bombs from aeroplanes," the dragon said. He sounded dazed.

"An aeroplane – " the parson began to explain.

"I know what an aeroplane is," the dragon snapped. "I have seen them when I am out flying."

"If you run into one with a swastika on its tail," the parson returned, "you might do us all a favor, and bring it down. They have been dropping bombs on London. The government is planning to send the children to the country to keep them safe. A whole orphanage would fit in this place."

It was only an idle thought when he said it, and yet in that instance it crystallized into a plan. The dragon saw it, and recoiled, neck frill rising.

"An *orphanage*!" the dragon cried.

"Children might be even more effective against your curse than a puppy," the parson said. "They can melt the hardest hearts. Look at Eppie in *Silas Marner* – " That surely had been published long after 1840. "Or Tiny Tim in *A Christmas Carol*?"

The dragon did not appear to recognize that reference either. He looked appalled. "Impossible," he said. "How could we let strangers into this place, when we are all – as we are? Would you banish me to the attics? Should I skulk around on the roof in the dark of night, so I can get some fresh air without being seen?"

"Not at all," the parson said. "I see no reason for you to hide yourself. I thought you might take it upon yourself to amuse the children."

"*Amuse* them," said the dragon, amazed. "My dear man, *look* at me." And he spread his wings, which spread so wide they all but filled the small breakfast room.

The parson paused, then rallied. "You would tell them you have some sort of queer disease," the parson said. "I daresay they'd get used to it – particularly if you took them flying."

"*Flying*," said the dragon. He sounded rather faint.

"We could make a little harness for you," the parson said. "So none of the children let go and fall, you know. It could be made quite safe."

"*Safe*." The dragon sounded like an affronted maiden aunt.

"Need I fetch the smelling salts?"

"No!" the dragon said. "No, this is all madness.

It could not possibly be done. We would have to hide, there would be no other choice; and no hiding place is proof against children."

"Not an orphanage, then," the parson returned. "A convalescent home. Sick men are not known for their dedication to exploration. But it seems to me an orphanage would be better. Children might thrust themselves on your notice."

"And why would I want children *thrusting themselves on my notice*?" the dragon demanded.

"It would give you something to do other than loaf in dark corners and brood."

"I do not sit around and brood!" the dragon roared. He struck his hands on the table, so his claws dug into the wood, and little licks of flame rose from his nose.

The parson waited impassively. The dragon settled back on his stool, his wings ruffling, and his neck frill still raised; and the parson said, "I know this is not to your taste, sir. But it seems to me that you must risk something, perhaps risk everything, if you are to break this curse."

The dragon's neck frill lowered. He was silent for a long time, and then he said, "It is too late to put your scheme in action. The enchantment will break on All Hallow's Eve this year, and there will be no enchanted meals to feed anyone after that, and perhaps not much of a house either. The enchantment's done all the upkeep. Without it, the house might fall to rack and ruin overnight. You may wake to discover the roof caved in, and a great oak tree grown up in the middle of the ballroom…"

The dolorous image seemed to please him. His

voice faded away, and he gazed into the middle distance, as if savoring it.

The possible wreck of the house did seem a fatal flaw in the orphanage scheme. The parson sighed. "Well," he said. "Then we must return to the puppy plan, then."

"Do you never give up?" the dragon asked. He sounded tired rather than angry now. "My heart is of solid stone, and incapable of melting."

"I shall not give up. Your servants' fates are yoked to yours, and for their sake I will continue to try no matter how hopeless you think you are. Even stone can melt."

The dragon blinked at him, a disconcerting lizard-blink where his lower eyelids rose.

"As soon as my leg is somewhat better," the parson said, "I shall go to the nearest village to find a puppy."

"You can leave whenever you want," the dragon said. He stood, his wings rearranging themselves in some dismay. "You need not pretend you shall come back."

"But I shall come back," the parson said.

The dragon flung up his clawed hands, and stalked from the breakfast room.

CHAPTER 8

It was nearly a week before the parson's leg was sound enough to allow him to carry out his scheme. The dragon did not warm to the idea, and refused to discuss it – refused, indeed, to discuss anything, but sat in brooding silence at breakfast each morning.

The rest of the day, he disappeared somewhere. "Up in his tower looking at his portrait from before, most like," Hugh said. "It's what he does mostly."

The parson choked on a laugh. "Does he now?"

"Oh, you're heartless, the lot of you," Annie scolded. "How's he to learn to love if we won't give him a bit of a chance?"

This seemed as good an opening as the parson was likely to get, so he said, "I thought he might start with a puppy."

"A puppy!" Mrs. Price cried.

"Why not? As far as I can tell, there is nothing in the curse that says he must learn romantic love. The witch did not ask him to marry her, did she? Only for alms."

A thoughtful hush fell among the servants. "A puppy, withal!" said Mrs. Price. She clicked her tongue. "I don't know as it would work. They don't have souls, the brute beasts."

"Now there I don't agree," the parson said mildly. "The good Lord made them all, just as He made you and me."

The parson did not think that he convinced them, but nonetheless when he asked where he might find a puppy, they gave him directions to the nearest village. "It's Briarfield. Lovely dances they had back in the day, too, don't you remember, Hugh?"

It was, they agreed, to the left down the road, and after that – a half mile, two miles? And was there a turning? They could not agree.

"The enchantment binds us to the estate," Annie said. "I tried and tried in the early days to get out at the gate, to go down to Briarfield to meet my Jimmy; but somehow the lane grew long, and turned in among the roses, and there I was back at the house again, and never even close to the outer wall."

"But it won't worry you, love," Mrs. Price said swiftly. "All our visitors have left easy as pie."

It was not fear for himself that had frozen the parson for a moment. It was the horror of a hundred years trapped in that spotless house and its endlessly blooming labyrinth of roses.

He swung his leg over the bicycle and began to pedal away down the clean white drive. "Good-bye!" the servants called after him. "Good-bye! Good-bye!"

And though the drive had looked endlessly long

at first, yet it seemed barely moments before the parson reached the iron gate and shot between the pillars into the forest.

The temperature did not change, nor the sunny weather, and yet there seemed a different quality to the air beyond the gates: the faint nutmeg scent of autumn, of leaves beginning to turn. September had arrived.

The parson drew in a deep breath of the soft air. The leaves rustled above his head, so the dappled sunlight on the dirt road shifted like a kaleidoscope. The parson felt like throwing back his head and singing into the sunshine, as he and Rupert Spiles used to do when they were students, and rode their bicycles through the countryside round Oxford to picnic in the long grass by the river.

Did students still ride their bicycles in the country, now that the war was on? Had Rose?

Rose!

The thought of Rose hit the parson with such force that he nearly careened into the stone wall by the side of the road. He stopped just in time, bent nearly double over her handlebars, gasping.

Rose, Rose, *Rose*! The parson had been missing – how long? Great Scott, he'd lost track of time. Could it be a week or more? His daughter must be wild with worry – indeed the whole village would be dismayed. *Kidnapped by German spies,* that's what they'd be saying: the parson knew his people.

How could he have been so thoughtless?

It was the enchantment: it had stolen his time and stolen his wits, and driven his daughter from his mind. He was on his bicycle again, he was pedaling

50

fast, flashing down the roadway with no eye for the dappled sun. He must ride back to Lesser Innsley at once, he must let them all know he was safe, and never return to those brutal roses and that enchanted estate and its ridiculous gloom-laden master, and leave them all to their doom –

He came to an abrupt stop again, and clung to his handlebars, breathing hard.

No. There was no one else coming; and Mrs. Price and Annie and Hugh were helpless to break the curse themselves. He could not simply abandon them to their fate – he could not even abandon the dragon to his. No.

He would write to his daughter. And then he would return to the estate.

The sunlight seemed dimmer as he rode slowly on. He reached the village of Briarfield swiftly, and found the little shop that was also the post office without trouble. He paused outside, girding himself – for a stranger's presence is always remarked in a village of this size, and he must offer some explanation for himself.

Well, he might very well say he was lost. His bicycle would certainly bear him up. Perhaps he might even say that he had passed an estate on the way into town – an estate surrounded by roses – and see if the local people could tell him anything that might be of use.

But the postmistress barely looked up from her book to count the parson's change when he bought his pen and ink and paper, and thus offered no opportunity for gentle interrogation. The parson retired to write, and then stopped, gazing down at the blank paper. What could he say?

Dearest Rose, I have stumbled on an enchanted estate, where a dragon who is also a man threatened to keep me prisoner. I have decided to stay and try to help him break his curse, because I feel sorry for his servants, who are cursed along with him, yet unlike him cannot break that curse on their own.

Well, that would convince Rose that her father had run mad.

In the end he wrote that he was well, and safe, and had fallen off his bicycle in the rain, and been too ill to write until now – which was not untrue, if one considered an enchantment a sort of illness. He would be staying where he was for now, and Rose was not to worry.

He could not recall Rose's latest address, so he wrote a similar letter to Miss Clarence, and enclosed the letter to Rose within. Miss Clarence could be counted upon to get the letter to its destination.

"I don't suppose," he asked the postmistress, when he came in to mail the letter, "that you know of any puppies in the village that might need a home? A fearless one," he added; it would need a fearless puppy indeed to warm to the dragon's lizard visage. "I have been detailed to find one to cheer up an invalid."

The postmistress's hitherto fixed gaze snapped up from her novel. She stared at the parson with ferocious intensity. "I know just the one."

***

It seemed a short ride indeed back to the estate. Worry ate away the miles. The dog sat in the parson's bicycle basket, her chin on its rim and her tongue lolling out so she could taste the wind on her face, and the parson kept glancing down at her, and wondering how the dragon would take to her – and if she would take to the dragon.

There was that subtle change in the air as he re-entered the iron gates: the smell of autumn replaced by the faint perfume of roses, the comfortable dirt track exchanged for the smooth-raked white gravel. His bicycle tires must have left a track as he rode out that morning, but even that had been smoothed away.

The dragon waited for him by the door.

The parson came to a stop perhaps ten feet from him. The dragon's wide-eyed gaze did not even flicker down to the little dog in the bicycle basket, but remained fixed on the parson. His wings flapped slowly, half-extended, as if he needed their support to balance.

"Well," said the parson, smiling, unnerved by this silent welcome. "I'm back."

"You're back," the dragon agreed.

"Saints be praised!" cried Annie, and the parson jumped at hearing her so near, when of course he could not see her. "None of the others came back. Not even Miss Granger."

The parson began to feel embarrassed. He pushed his bicycle forward, so that the dog in the bicycle basket was nearly under the dragon's nose. The dog peered upward, her soft chestnut fur obscuring her eyes. She gave a thoughtful sniff, and then a friendly little bark, and the parson ruffled her soft floppy ears.

"I brought you a dog," the parson said. "As I promised. Her name is Daisy."

The dragon blinked, his lower eyelids lifting in that odd reptilian way, and looked down. Daisy looked back up at him, bright-eyed, the reddish glints in her long soft fur gleaming in the sun.

"You promised me a puppy," the dragon said.

The parson sighed. "So I did. But the postmistress needed a home for her late mother's dog, and… I thought the act of charity might tell against the curse… and after all, a puppy would need to be trained."

"I know how to train a puppy," the dragon snapped.

Of course he did. That was the sort of thing they learned on these country estates. The parson sighed. "Will you not stroke her ears?"

The dragon reached out – quite as carefully as if he thought the little dog might bite him, as if her teeth would have any chance against his scaly hide – and stroked the pads of his fingers down Daisy's ears. The dog gave her head a shake, and licked the dragon's palm. He jerked his hand back.

"You should feed her," the parson advised. "You should be the only one who feeds her. I have seen shell-shocked soldiers make great, great strides when they are given charge of a dog."

The dragon had been reaching for the dog again, but now his hand paused in midair. Daisy stretched out her nose toward him, trying to sniff his claws. "I am not a soldier," the dragon objected.

"I have seen many people who have suffered," the parson said, "return to life and love and happiness through the agency of a good dog. Do try."

The dragon reached out, his arms fully extended, and lifted the dog from the basket. His wary expression turned to one of confusion as he lifted the dog further, and then to horror – for Daisy's hind legs were mere stumps.

An accident with a lawnmower, the postmistress had said. "A sovereign dog for an invalid," she had said, almost pleading. "She can't get up and run off." And she had turned away, with the swiftness of an Englishwoman who could not quite repress her tears – and then Daisy had sniffed the parson's palm with her soft nose, and the parson could not resist her.

"You brought me a defective dog!" the dragon roared.

"Don't drop her!"

Even as the parson shouted, Daisy fell – but only a little: invisible hands caught her in midair, and Annie cried, "There now! I've got you!" And Daisy began to sniff the invisible arms, and wagged the stub of her once-plumy tail.

All at once the parson was overcome with exasperation. "My good man," he told the dragon, his voice clipped with suppressed fury. "She's your last chance. And I will remind you that you are hardly a prize yourself, and are not the only one who will be cursed forever if you can't even bring yourself to try!"

Smoke billowed from the dragon's nostrils. The parson braced himself for an eruption, and prepared to meet the dragon glare for glare and shout for shout, if necessary.

But the dragon did not shout. He breathed in and out, heavily, smoke puffing from his nose. Then, very slowly, his shoulders set with injured dignity, he gingerly took Daisy from Annie's hands, and held the dog away from him, rather as if he expected her to bite.

The parson's anger evaporated into a desire to laugh. He resisted it. The dragon would not understand, and the parson did not want to hurt him. "She will not hurt you, you know," the parson said.

"I am not afraid of that," the dragon said stiffly. Daisy attempted to lick his hand. "I kept hunting dogs – long ago – " Daisy barked, her tail stump wagging. The dragon shuddered. "It was a very long time ago."

"Well," said the parson, "You had better hold that dog closer to you – like a baby." The dragon looked at him, appalled. Clearly a man who had never held a baby. "Like so," said the parson, and demonstrated with his own arms, making a movement as if to cradle something to his chest. The dragon copied him gingerly. "And now we had better take her inside, and see what there is to eat," the parson instructed. "I at least am famished; and I imagine Daisy must be, as well."

CHAPTER 9

The dragon brought Daisy to breakfast each morning, and fed her kippers from his plate with a solicitousness that almost made the parson want to laugh, although he restrained himself. One might laugh at a baby as it takes its first wobbling steps – a baby will not be discouraged – but a grown-up man, wobbling on his feet as he rose from his sick bed, would feel ashamed, and might refuse to try again.

On the third day, the dragon informed the parson, "I am still a dragon."

"Well," said the parson, "so you don't love Daisy yet. You can't expect it to happen all at once."

The dragon patted the dog's head. "I don't suppose I look any less dragon-ish," he said; "perhaps about the snout?"

The parson peered and was forced to admit that, alas, he did not. "But," he said, "it is not truly love, you know, if you are trying to feel it purely for the selfish purpose of breaking the curse."

"Selfish," the dragon said, and slouched on his stool. "It's not selfish. I would not try at all, if it only concerned myself. I am only trying now for the sake of my servants." Daisy put her paws on the table and sniffed hopefully in the direction of the parson's toast. The dragon put his hand on her head and pushed her back in his lap. "This isn't going to work," the dragon said.

The parson tore off a corner of toast and handed it to the dragon to feed to the dog. "Then at least then you shall have the satisfaction of shouting 'I told you so!' when All Hallow's Eve has come, if the curse remains unbroken."

The dog changed the dragon's habits in other ways, too. He no longer disappeared all day to brood, but reappeared morning, noon, and night to carry Daisy into the rose garden, so that the little dog might answer the call of nature.

The parson made it his business to be in the garden as well at those times, on the grounds that a friendly human presence might induce the dragon to linger longer in the fresh air and the sunshine – which might put him in a better frame of mind for learning how to love.

In truth, the parson was rather surprised to find the dragon trying so hard. He had expected the dragon to give up quickly, perhaps even to refuse to try, as he had refused to even meet many of the young ladies his servants brought to the estate.

But perhaps the nearness of the curse's end had spurred him to action.

Whatever the reason, he *was* trying. The parson did most of the talking, and the dragon ruffled his wings and snorted smoke through his nose – but nonetheless, generally he landed close by the parson, when he could have flown Daisy anywhere in that labyrinth of a rose garden, and avoided human conversation entirely.

One evening found the parson sitting on a stone bench, an ebony walking stick that he had found in the library resting next to him. The dragon stood a few feet away, and they both watched Daisy snuffling at the lawn. It seemed a perfectly ordinary patch of lawn to the parson; but the dog pulled herself forward with her forelegs, sniffing happily at the ground, following some trail invisible to human eyes.

"Do you know," the parson commented, "when I was a young man, someone told me that dogs cannot see color. For a long time after that, I felt sorry for them; but then I began to wonder if perhaps dogs do not feel sorry for us, because to them it must seem that our sense of smell is entirely lacking. It is as if we are all blind, or deaf. I wonder if they try to speak to us in their own way, using smells, only to find us utterly insensible to it. Do you think they worry about our incapacity?"

The dragon was staring at him. "What?"

"I think they must," the parson said. "I do not think it is in dogs to feel superior because they can do what we cannot – the way that we feel superior about our spoken language, and scoff that dogs only understand a few words, when we cannot understand even that much of their language of smells. I think our limitations must move them to compassion."

"You think too much," the dragon scoffed.

"Probably," the parson agreed, quite cheerfully. "But still you must admit that a dog is a more loving creature than man. All the things that we wish we were, dogs are: loyal, faithful, loving, and cheerful in the face of adversity. Look at Daisy," he said, and gestured at the dog, who was ecstatically sniffing a tussock of grass. "She has lost both her hind legs, and yet – "

The dragon dragged his clawed foot through the dirt. "So I ought to be more like a dog, is that it?"

"Rare is the man of whom that could not be said. Certainly it could be said of me," the parson said, and he tapped his bad leg with the ebony walking stick. "This injury is twenty years old, and yet still sometimes I brood on the things it will not let me do. What good is that? You will never catch a dog doing it. They are the true Stoics."

The dragon did not answer. The parson thought that perhaps he was not listening, but then the dragon said, rather awkwardly, "I have always been very fond of dogs. We had a great many when I was young, but after Father died the place was mismanaged, and most of the dogs sold off. I meant to breed a pack again, after I came of age."

He sounded as if he meant to go on, but he did not. The parson said, to encourage him, "Did you have a favorite dog?"

"Bella," the dragon said. "My pointer bitch. She died while I was away at school." And then, abruptly, as if to turn the conversation, he pointed at the parson's polished ebony walking stick, with its carven ivory handle. "Is that mine?"

The parson rested a hand on it lightly. "It is. There was rain last night and sometimes that stiffens my leg, so I have borrowed this cane for the day."

"You should have asked."

"You were not by to ask," the parson said. "I only found it this afternoon. Is it a part of your hoard?"

"I have no hoard."

"Oh? So if someone came into this house, and made away with – say – a single rose, such as you would never miss – you would not fly after them huffing and puffing and boiling with rage?"

The dragon's wings ruffled irritably. "That's just standing on my rights as an Englishman," he said. "Old Mr. Henry used to come after us with his musket when we scrumped his apples – my cousins and I."

"So Englishmen are all dragons," the parson said. "But I expect Mr. Henry didn't attempt to kidnap you."

"*He* was not under a curse," the dragon responded. "I was quite desperate – quite desperate."

And certainly the parson knew from the trenches that desperate men took desperate measures. He rested his chin on the cool ivory handle of the cane, and let the topic lapse.

"I'm sorry," the dragon said suddenly.

The parson was obscurely touched. "Well enough," he said. "Just see that you don't do it again."

The dragon did not answer.

Daisy made a little whining noise in her throat, which was the sound she made when she had grown tired, and wanted to be picked up. The dragon, well-trained, went to her and lifted her in his arms. His wings mantled, and drew inward, encircling himself with the tired dog in his arms. It reminded the parson unexpectedly of his own wife Emily, in her youth, holding baby Rose in her arms.

The dragon settled his wings again, and looked over at the parson's soft smile, and frowned. "Why have you stayed?" he asked abruptly.

The parson blinked, and straightened. "I suppose I feel I have a duty here," he said.

"A duty," the dragon said, and there was some bitterness in his voice. "I suppose you feel as a man of God that it is your duty to redeem me."

"I would not presume so much," the parson replied. "It is for God to redeem."

The dragon snorted through his nose, blowing dark puffs of smoke. He turned away from the garden and went back toward the house, walking swiftly enough that the parson made no attempt to keep up.

And yet the next morning, he was back, bringing Daisy out with the sun. He and the parson sat side by side without speaking, watching the dog inspect the dewy spider webs on the lawn.

CHAPTER 10

Perhaps some of the magic of the estate clung to the letter. It took far longer than it ought to have done to get to Miss Clarence, and by the time it arrived the village had quite given him up for dead. "Killed by a German spy for his bicycle," was the verdict in the Green Man. "Threw his body in the swamp, most like, and rode off neat as you please."

The rumors had gained such force that even the arrival of the letter did not kill them, but only changed their form. Kidnapped rather than killed, he'd been, and snuck a letter out somehow (a game chap, their parson; they were proud of him in Lesser Innsley). "Have you held the letter over a lamp, Miss? That's how you get invisible ink to show," the schoolchildren anxiously informed Miss Clarence.

Miss Clarence pooh-poohed their suggestions. She sent the enclosed letter on to Rose and firmly declared the matter closed. She was not of a suspicious cast of mind: she did not read detective fiction, and scoffed at stories of spies.

But despite her loud scoffing, the vagueness of the letter and the lack of a return address gnawed at her. One rainy evening, sitting in front of her fire and rereading *Nicholas Nickleby*, Miss Clarence found herself not reading at all but gazing into the flames, listening to the rain on the roof and worrying.

A knock interrupted her worries. Miss Clarence closed her book smartly and hastened toward the door, and opened it to find – "Rose!"

"I came as soon as I could get leave," Rose said. The color was high in her cheeks, and Miss Clarence's mind at once jumped to visions of pneumonia. She bustled Rose into the house and out of her coat and into Miss Clarence's own pet chair before the fire, with an afghan Miss Clarence's sister had crocheted around her knees, and a cup of tea beside her.

"We must go find my father," Rose said, which she had said three times before, only to be informed severely that it was no good finding her father if Rose died of pneumonia straightaway thereafter.

"But Rose, dear, how can we?" Miss Clarence said. "There's no return address."

"Have you kept the envelope?" Rose asked.

"Yes," Miss Clarence said reluctantly. Usually she tided envelopes away as spills for fires, but this one she had preserved, although she could not explain to herself why. "But, as I said, there is no…"

Rose snatched the envelope from her hand. "But there is a postmark! We'll follow it back, and see if we can discover anything else about it. I hope the postmistress is an inveterate gossip. They always are in books."

Miss Clarence gazed at her, exasperation mingled with admiration. The admiration won; and a smile illuminated Miss Clarence's face. "I suppose," she allowed, "mystery novels are not an utterly valueless form of literature after all. Is the village on the train?"

Rose shook her head. "But it doesn't matter," she said triumphantly. "One of my chums lent me a motorcycle with a sidecar. We shall take that tomorrow morning."

"A sidecar!" Miss Clarence said faintly. But at once she despised that faintheartedness: who was she to fear a ride in a sidecar when an old friend was in danger? "We shall start in the morning, then," she pronounced.

"That's the spirit!" Rose cried.

But even this heroic mood could not overcome Miss Clarence's basic practicality. "If the weather clears."

"It had better," Rose said.

***

The parson climbed up to the third floor that morning. He wanted to look out of the high windows, and get a view of the countryside all round, and see if the trees beyond the walls had begun to turn yellow. It did not seem to him that the walls were so very high: yet it was impossible to see the forest beyond them, when one stood among the roses.

The trees had indeed turned yellow, touched with red and brown: beyond the enchantment, autumn was come. The parson lifted his chin and trained his eyes on the golden trees, and tried to realize in his heart that the summer had gone.

It was then that he heard the sound of wheels on the gravel drive. He peered down through the window. A motorcycle with a sidecar drove up the white lane, and sitting astride, very smart in a blue skirt suit –

Rose.

Rose had come to the dragon's lair.

The parson rushed for the stairs. He should not run, his bad leg could scarcely stand it; and normally that did not bother him, but in that moment the parson would have sacrificed a fatted calf only to be able to fly down the stairs and shout to his daughter, "Turn back! Turn back!"

But the fatted calf would have died in vain, for by the time the parson reached the grand staircase, the dragon stood already at its foot. The parson let out an inarticulate cry, and the dragon twisted away from the door to gaze up in astonishment as the parson hurried down the stairs.

The dragon rose to the half-landing with a flap of his wings. The parson stopped on the far side, and they stood with that expanse between them. The dragon's wings spread, cutting off the stairs entirely, and blocking all view of the door. Curls of flames licked up from his snout.

"Whom have you summoned?" the dragon demanded.

"Let me pass," the parson said.

A gout of flame flared from the dragon's nose. "Tell me!" he shouted

The parson met him rage for rage. "I have summoned no one," he said. "They have come of their own free will. Now let me go, so I can tell her to leave!"

Another knock. The parson flinched as if pricked by a pin, his eyes darting to the door despite the dragon looming in front of him.

"Your daughter," the dragon said, with a quick leap of intuition. "It is your daughter who is come."

The parson started forward, as if he meant to push the dragon down the stairs. If he would have done it, he never knew; for the dragon danced aside, pressing himself against the railing and gazing at the parson with the whites showing around his eyes, though the parson was half his size.

Fear gave way to indignation. The dragon's frill bristled, and he snarled, "How dare you think I am any threat to her?"

"How dare *I*? You *have* threatened her!" the parson said.

"It was weeks ago!"

"And you have never withdrawn those threats," the parson interrupted. "Are you surprised I have little faith in you? What in your conduct ought to incline me to have any?"

"After all I have done for that stupid dog – !" the dragon exploded.

"I have known bad men who have loved their dogs," the parson shot back. "Promise me safe conduct for Rose."

The dragon ruffled his wings. His bristling frill rose higher, and then flattened back again, and his long jaw clenched. "Very well," the dragon said, all his old sulkiness in his voice. "Your daughter – indeed the whole party – will leave unharmed whenever they like. I give you my word."

The parson essayed a bow, because he did not think that he could say anything that would not sound sarcastic. And he went on past the dragon, aware as he did it how much larger the dragon was than himself: how tall he was, how vast his shoulders, how strong his arms. He had lifted the parson to the roof with no trouble at all when the parson had tried to take a rose.

"I could never love her anyway," the dragon growled.

The parson paused to look back. The dragon propelled himself upward, toward the high ceiling, and then disappeared around the curve of the stairs, and was gone.

The parson felt the weakness that follows after battle shivering through his limbs. He had to grip the rail to keep himself from falling, and it surprised him at every step that his weak knees could hold him.

He saw now how hopeless his first plan would have been. If he had run outside waving his arms and shouting "Go back! Go back!" was it likely that Rose would have listened? No; and indeed Miss Clarence was a firm and stubborn soul as well. They would have become only more determined to stay and discover what was wrong.

The parson was on the penultimate step when the

sound of the knocker reverberated through the house. It seemed to set off a chorus of echoes, although they were not echoes, quite, but the sounds of the servants whispering. It had been a very long time since any guests had come to the front door.

"I will open it," the parson said, and thought he heard Hugh groan with disappointment. "If you will please set up a tea for us in the back gardens in an hour's time, that would be very kind."

The whispering grew louder, happier now, and the parson had the impression of... movement, perhaps; nothing so definite as shapes in the air; indeed once the impression was gone, the parson thought perhaps it was nothing but a trick of the light.

The knocker sounded again, more firmly, as if the next step might be a battering ram. The parson hurried the last few steps to the heavy door, and dragged it open.

And there, on the porch, stood his Rose.

"Dad!" she cried, and the relief in her face brought tears to his eyes.

"I worried you, my dear. I am sorry."

They were not hugging people. But the parson took her hand in both his own, and held it between them; and they smiled at each other.

***

Of course Miss Clarence had to be greeted as well, and hands shaken all around, and apologies given for the fact that the parson could not give them a tour of the house: "The owner is a great recluse," the parson explained. "He does not like having people about. But we will have tea in the garden, in an hour."

It might have taken a little doing to dispatch Miss Clarence, but she was a discreet soul, and dispatched herself for them by announcing her intention of finding that sweet gazebo whose roof peeked above the rose hedges. "Don't pick the roses," the parson warned, with more urgency than he intended: "The master of the house is possessive of them."

"Well of course I should not go picking someone else's roses," Miss Clarence said. The parson smiled weakly.

And then Rose and her father were alone, and walked together in another branch of the garden. Rose said, "We thought you must be hurt, or ill. Why have you not come home?"

The question chagrined the parson. "They looked after me when I was ill…" he began.

But then his mind went blank. Only his affair with Rupert Spiles had ever put him in a position where he must tell elaborate lies, and that was so long ago that he was entirely out of practice.

And in any case, he hated to lie to his daughter. But neither could he speak with absolute honesty ("The master of the house kidnapped me and now I feel sorry for him"?), so he took refuge in partial truth. "The master of the house is very ill," he explained. "It cheers him to have me near. I felt that it was my duty to stay."

"But you have a duty to Lesser Innsley, too," Rose said. Her voice was not sharp, but now that her initial relief was over, the parson heard a creeping disappointment in her tone.

"I know," he said, befuddled, because in fact the magic of the place had pushed that duty very far from his mind. "I do know, my dear. I do not know how to explain…" And here he paused, grasping for some explanation that would suffice, and would not require bringing in magic and curses and generally sounding quite mad.

But he could think of nothing. "He asked me to stay till the end of October," he said finally. "The… the doctors think that his disease will reach a crisis by then, and his fate decided one way or another. I did not feel I could say no. Do you understand?"

He looked at Rose's face then. She was biting her lip, her smooth young forehead creased, her eyes troubled; but as he watched, her forehead smoothed, and she reached out and touched his sleeve. "I don't," she said frankly. "But I do believe that if you are doing it, then it must be right."

The parson was so touched that he could not speak for some moments. "Thank you," he said. "I am afraid you may overrate your old father, but – I thank you."

They walked in silence for a while. A late bumblebee alighted on a rose, and the parson eyed it thoughtfully. He could not recall seeing insects in the garden before. And indeed the house itself seemed suspiciously free of mice…

"I am afraid this visit won't last long," Rose said. "We must leave in time to be back before dark."

"Of course," the parson said. "I shouldn't like you driving these winding roads without headlights." For headlights, like all other lights in the night, were not to be shown for the duration. "However did you get enough petrol?"

"Oh," said Rose, and she smiled. "The whole village clubbed together – everyone who gets a petrol ration. They are all very worried about you, Father."

And the parson was again painfully touched, and again aghast at how little thought he had given Lesser Innsley since he had gone. It did not seem right than even an enchantment should make him so forgetful. "You must tell them," he said at last, and his voice was gruff, "that I am truly thankful. Truly thankful, my dear Rose."

And there was nothing more to say on that topic: so for a time they did not say anything, but only wandered along a lane of roses, which drooped heavy and scented from the pergola above their heads.

They came through the lane to one of the rose-hedged circles. Rose turned slowly to look at it. "They are truly splendid for roses so late in the season," she said, and went to smell one, a vast blooming cabbage head of a rose. It made her sneeze, and she gave her head a shake, and turned to look searchingly at her father. "You are happy here?" she said. "Your invalid sounds..." She paused, as though searching for a word that was not insulting, and yet would get her point across. "Eccentric," she said at last.

"I am happy here," the parson assured her, and added, quite truthfully, "Happier now that I have seen you. I'm sorry that I worried you."

But Rose was still troubled. "Why didn't you include a return address?" she asked. "We all would have been so much easier in our minds had we known where you were – and it would have been so much easier to find you if we could simply have said, Briarley Estate."

The truth was that it had not occurred to the parson, and he was baffled at that omission as soon as she mentioned it. One always included a return address, and also wrote the place of writing just below the date in a letter; and yet he had not done so.

Part of the magic of the place, perhaps. A secret enchanted estate would not want its existence brandished about on an envelope.

"I am so sorry," he said helplessly. "How did you find me without the address?"

"We followed the postmark to the village and asked after you at the post office, where the postmistress told us the story of the man who had adopted her crippled dog – and of course we knew that had to be you," Rose said, so wryly that the parson laughed.

"Surely I am not so bad as all that."

"You have an incorrigible affection for broken things," Rose teased. "It is a sickness with you. Why, I've seen you take dented canned goods because you felt sorry for the can."

The parson laughed as he had not laughed in a good long while. "My darling girl, how I've missed you," he said.

"You could come away with us," Rose said. She lifted her eyes to his face.

The parson dropped his own gaze. He was tempted, powerfully tempted. But even in that moment, he knew he could not possibly say yes. Yet it was very hard to speak.

"My dear girl," he said at last. "No. I have made promises: I have a duty here."

Rose sighed, but made no other remonstrance. "Well," she said. "At least I shall get a proper address for this place before I go. Do you know, no one could tell us where it was? Even the postman, who delivers here, took some time before he could remember the road to follow."

Her tone was jocular, but her eyes were questioning again. And yet the parson had no answer he could give. "Memory works in odd ways," he said, with a false heartiness. "And you found it in the end, at any rate."

Rose assented with a nod. They walked together, side by side, much as they used to in the garden at the parsonage; but it was not the old companionable silence that hung between them, and that grieved the parson, the more because he did not know how to fix it. His answers to her questions had been evasive, but what else could he say?

But she slipped her hand through his arm, as she had when she was younger, and he looked at her with some surprise, and smiled at her.

"I rather enjoyed playing detective," Rose said, "now that it has turned out all right, of course. Don't give me a reason to do it again." And she made a bulldog face at him, which made him laugh.

The rose hedges herded them over to Miss Clarence's gazebo just as the silvery sound of a triangle tinkled over the garden to call them to tea. They all three set out together, and made their way out of the rose labyrinth in a remarkably short time (the parson noticed Rose's brow wrinkling again), and walked around to the back of the house where tea had been set waiting for them in the sunshine.

"Oh my good gracious!" Miss Clarence cried.

This from Miss Clarence was practically a profanity: and in that moment the parson saw the tea table through her eyes, and nearly passed out himself. For the servants had laid out a *real tea*, with golden scones and golden butter, and a little silver pitcher of fresh cream, and a bowl of pure white sugar lumps: such a spread as one could not find in all of England in those days of rationing.

"My goodness gracious!" Miss Clarence cried again, her hand to her heart. "How can this be?"

CHAPTER 11

In his own war, the parson had learned the trick of swift decisions, and he made one in this moment. There was no explanation for this that would suffice, except the truth. Sensible Miss Clarence was the last person one would wish to tell a tale of enchantment, yet it must be done.

"I will fetch the servants," the parson said. "And they will explain all."

"Indeed we're all right here," said Annie, and she sounded close to tears. "Didn't we make the right thing for the tea? Oh, it's my fault; Mrs. Price thought we ought to make proper buns or even a syllabub, but I said scones are so fast, and newfangled too, made with bicarbonate of soda…"

Mrs. Price's voice rose out of the air. "I suppose that's not so new anymore."

Miss Clarence had grabbed onto the back of a wicker chair, and grasped it with both hands. "Goodness gracious," she said; and Rose managed to pull out the chair beside just in time for Miss

Clarence to fall down into it.

"Dad," Rose said. "What's happening?"

"I'm afraid I've rather sprung this on you," the parson said. "But I believe you would have thought me dotty if I tried to explain this any other way. You see, there's a curse – "

All in all, the tale went down more readily than the parson could have guessed. Though in the normal way of things Miss Clarence scorned to believe in ghoulies and ghosties and things that go bump in the night, her good sturdy common sense would not let her refuse the evidence of her own senses. "I don't wish to be a doubting Thomas," she said, rather apologetically, as the explanation reached the enchantress's curse and the invisible servants; "but all the same…"

"Ma'am," said Mrs. Price, "I haven't spear wounds you can probe, but if it would help you to touch my hand, I'll gladly give it."

"Yes," said Miss Clarence. She held out her hand. "If you will – Oh!" And her hand jerked back and her eyes grew wide at that invisible touch.

"Now let's get you a nice cup of tea," said Mrs. Price. "That'll set you right in a moment." The teapot rose from its place, and poured into a delicate china cup. "Do you take sugar, love?"

Miss Clarence's hands grasped claw-like on the wicker chair arms. "One lump," she said, and if her voice was rather faint, it was at least steady.

Under the influence of tea, she recovered quickly. And Rose shook Mrs. Price's hand as well, and listened seriously as the servants spoke of their hundred years of waiting – the long parade of girls –

the parson's novel idea for a puppy.

"Dad," she said, rather hesitantly, as the explanation wound to its close. "Wouldn't it be better if I took your place? If the dog hasn't broken the curse yet, well then, maybe it *is* romantic after all."

"No." It was not the parson who answered: he was too aghast to speak. Miss Clarence stepped manfully into the breach. "Absolutely not, Rose," she said firmly. "You have your war work."

"But any girl could do that, really," Rose said.

"And you're a pretty thing," Annie added, quite unhelpfully, the parson felt. "It *might* work."

"Rose!" Miss Clarence sounded shocked. "You can't abandon your country in the hour of her greatest need. My dear girl, you would be declared AWOL!"

Rose's eye took on a mulish gleam. This was the wrong tack to take, the parson felt: there would be something appealing to Rose in the idea of breaking the rules for the sake of some greater good.

"You are meant for better things than to turn your life over to a beast of a man who doesn't give a fig about girls," Miss Clarence added warmly.

The words seemed to kick open a door in the parson's head: a door that perhaps should have been open before, given his own history, and yet it was only now that the possibility occurred to him.

I could not love her, the dragon had said.

Now the parson would be the first to admit that his partiality to his daughter might cloud his vision. But it seemed to him that if the dragon *could not* love Rose, could not even entertain the possibility

78

of doing so –

Well. If he could not love Rose, then surely he could not love any woman.

Perhaps he inclined toward men.

Those thoughts flashed through the parson's mind in a moment, and the possibility burgeoned almost to a certainty. The dragon's servants had trooped past him a hundred years of girls, and the curse had not been broken, because the dragon was homosexual.

Did the word homosexual even exist in 1840? The parson did not think it had. A sodomite, that was the word they would have used. The dragon was a sodomite, and so ashamed that he could not tell his servants, even though his silence ensured that the curse would remain unbroken, and the dragon and all his servants trapped until the end.

The parson felt a queer sense of revulsion at the dragon's selfishness – and yet understanding too: he had felt that shame, and knew its overmastering power. Who knew how it might have deformed his own life if he had not known Rupert Spiles?

"My dear," the parson cut in – for Rose and Miss Clarence had continued to argue as all this passed through his mind. "My darling girl. It would not work."

Rose faltered, and looked at her father, frowning at the firmness of his voice. The parson gazed at her steadily, willing her to understand him. He could not think how to explain to her without telling Annie and Mrs. Price, as well, and despite everything he felt he ought to keep the dragon's secrets.

"It could!" Annie cried, and there was a thread of desperation in her voice. "*Couldn't* it, now? Don't you think he give it a proper chance just this once, now that it's so late?"

"Och, he's too sunk in his despair for any such thing," Mrs. Price replied. "It's a sweet offer, girl, but it's too late. You'd best go on now, and convince your father to go too if he can, or else maybe the house'll drag him right down to Hell with the rest of us when the time comes."

Rose's head had turned toward Annie's voice, and then toward Mrs. Price's, and now she looked back at her father. The parson took both her hands. "My dear, go back to your work," he told her. He had thought how to tell her, now. "Do you recall that schoolmate you so disliked – that Oscar Wilde? Could he have loved you if it would have saved him from a curse?"

A moment of uncertainty; and then understanding flooded Rose's face. "All right," she said. "But there's nothing you can do either, then. Won't you come away with us, Dad?"

"We need you sorely in Lesser Innsley," Miss Clarence added.

The parson smiled and shook his head and removed his hands from his daughter's. "I made a promise," he said. "And I still have some hope that the dog will work her magic. Now come," he said. "I know it has been months since you have seen such a tea as this; and it will be months at least, years probably, before you see such a tea again. Do your duty by it."

And indeed, they did the tea full justice. They

drained the pot, and ate the scones down to the crumbs, spread lavishly with butter and jam. Rose actually clapped her hands when a floating tray appeared from the house, carrying sandwiches made of the good roast beef, and Hugh's voice – gruff with shyness – said, "Eat up."

The shadows grew long by the time they had eaten themselves to repletion. "We ought to try taking some of the provisions out of the estate," Rose said. "Just think what a boon an endless supply of butter and roast beef could be! Even if the supply only lasts until the All Hallow's Eve – " And she stopped, embarrassed, and her gaze flickered toward Mrs. Price's floating teacup.

The cup laid itself gently back in its saucer. "As it will," Mrs. Price said. "One way or another."

They packed up a good block of butter in a napkin, for Rose and Miss Clarence to take home, and see if it vanished like fairy gold. The light was westering now, and they must leave soon if they hoped to get home before dark; and so the tea party broke up, and they went back to the drive.

The motorcycle did not want to start. Rose tinkered with it, and Miss Clarence sat next to the parson on a stone bench tucked in beside the house. "Are you sure you will not come back with us?" she asked.

"I do not think that motorcycle will accommodate three," the parson said lightly.

"Be serious," she scolded him. "I simply do not see what good you can do by staying here. I feel quite doubtful that you are correct in your understanding of the curse."

"I don't see why," the parson replied. "The enchantress asked for supper, not for the master of the house to plight his troth to her. Romantic love had nothing to do with the laying of the curse. Why then should it take romantic love to break it?"

"Very sound Oxford logic," Miss Clarence said drily. "You are thinking of love as *you* understand it, as an educated man of God. But you are not the one who laid the curse: it was an enchantress, who must have been a vengeful woman, to consider a hundred years an appropriate punishment for a single evening of unkindness. What would she consider love?"

"It is a little more than unkindness to turn one of God's creatures away hungry into the cold," the parson said.

"Yes, of course," Miss Clarence said, with deceptive mildness. The parson sighed. Despite his quibble, her bolt had struck home, and when he tried to dislodge it from his mind, it only sunk in more deeply.

"You are right," the parson said, and wished he could add *damn you*. "Vengeful indeed. The dragon might open his heart to an entire orphanage of children and that might not suffice to break the enchantress's curse. What would such a woman mean when she said love? I will not – " And here the parson lowered his voice. "I will *not* have Rose staying here."

"No," Miss Clarence agreed. "It would be useless." And then she added, disapproving: "Was it wise to let her read Oscar Wilde?"

"She is nursing the war-wounded in a hospital,

82

Miss Clarence," the parson said equitably. "She will come upon things far worse than Mr. Wilde."

Miss Clarence sighed. They sat, watching Rose fiddled with the motorcycle's engine, and the parson wondered dispiritedly if the enchantress's definition of love were wide enough to encompass a romantic love that was *not* a man's love for a woman. It did not seem very likely.

"Indeed, perhaps I'm wrong," Miss Clarence said. "Perhaps you are quite right to believe that the love of Christian charity will serve as well as any to break the curse."

"Let us hope," the parson said. "Time grows so short, I do not see that there is much chance of anything else now, even if Rose did stay and – things were quite other than what they are."

The motorcycle grumbled to life. Rose swung it around so Miss Clarence might climb into the sidecar, and as Miss Clarence arranged herself, Rose said to her father, "You are sure you don't wish to come along? There is room for you on this seat."

"I am sure, my dear," the parson said.

But his heart had grown heavy, and Rose must have heard it in his voice, for she looked anxiously in his face. "You *will* be all right?"

"My dear, you are the one who is going to war," the parson said gently.

"Yes," Rose agreed, rather truculently; and rallied to say, "So you see why it is important that I need not worry about you. It might distract me from my war work, and then where would we be?"

"Very sad indeed, no doubt," the parson said.

"But I assure you, there is no need of that. I will be very well here."

"I will pray for you," Rose said.

"And I for you," the parson said.

"Indeed, we both shall," Miss Clarence said. She buckled her helmet firmly on her head, and gave a nod to Rose.

The parson stood in the drive and waved as Rose and Miss Clarence drove away. He remained there as the sun lowered, and the shadows lengthened, and the raked white drive gleamed like a river of gold in the lowering afternoon light.

CHAPTER 12

The parson's leg had begun to ache from his long day's exertion, but still he did not walk directly back to the house. He walked in the rose gardens instead, and got lost among the hedges, with their deep red roses nearly black in the gathering dusk. The thought Miss Clarence had planted had taken firm root in the parson's mind: and now that it was growing there, he must see if he could make it bear fruit.

In short, he must find some way to discuss it with the dragon.

Homosexuality seemed a delicate subject to bring up with a dragon-man who was inclined to blow fire from his nostrils when he felt insulted – as he surely would if the parson's supposition were wrong, and even perhaps if it were right.

But could a man who was ashamed, who might very well hate himself, learn to love? The parson had known such men at Oxford, had tried to counsel such among his parishioners. He had felt that shame himself in his youth, before he had known Rupert Spiles, who had helped him to look at such things in a new light – before Rupert himself had been extinguished at Passchendaele.

The parson walked slowly, his hands clasped behind his back, so deep in thought and so far from decision that he did not notice the dragon sitting on one of the ornamental benches until the dragon said, "Good evening."

Then the parson rose from his brown study. It had grown quite dark without him noticing: the stars began to be visible in the sky. "Good evening," the parson said.

"Did you enjoy your daughter's visit?" the dragon asked.

"Very much," the parson said.

The dragon did not say anything else, but he looked at the parson expectantly, so that the parson waited instead of walking on. But the dragon did not speak, and at length the parson spoke instead.

"I think there will be frost tonight," he said, and the dragon lowered his head in assent. "Will it kill the roses?"

The dragon looked surprised. "Of course not," he said, and then he was silent and thoughtful. "I suppose most roses die in winter," he murmured to himself.

After a hundred years of ever-blooming roses, one might very well forget that. The silence fell between them. The parson inspected the roses again.

"No one missed me when I had gone," the dragon said.

The parson drew back from the roses to look at the dragon. The moon rose behind him, casting his face in shadow, but outlining the slump-shouldered silhouette of his body. His wings rose high and protective about him.

"The servants told me they sent out invitations to your neighbors," the parson said. "And yet when they came, you hid in the dungeon and would not see them."

The dragon looked stunned, and then his neck frill bristled with anger, and brief curls of fire rose from his nostrils. But he did not shout, and after some time his frill smoothed over again, and he ran a hand over his head, and looked sheepish.

"Perhaps it is so," he said. "But they did not come back later."

"Perhaps they thought you had gone away," the parson said. "Shut up the house and gone to the continent. Why should they visit an empty house?" The dragon did not look convinced. "And the enchantment makes it hard for people to remember the estate, I think," the parson ventured.

But the dragon shook his head. "The servants were not all forgotten. Some had families come to look for them, or friends."

The parson turned away, because the moon was full in his face, and he did not want the dragon to see his feelings. He thought of those families coming to find their lost children – imagined Rose going away in service, and disappearing – and the magic ensuring he never knew where or how.

"It is a cruel curse," the parson said.

"No." The dragon's voice was dull. "For when

someone who loved them came, the servants shed their invisibility, and could go home with them. That is why there are only three left."

This seemed to the parson almost crueler – at least to the ones who were left; and he found he did not know what to say. So he did not respond directly. "Come," the parson said. "Walk with me."

The dragon heaved himself to his feet, and they walked on through the endless hedges of roses, which should have been withering in that chill air. Soon the frost would come, and beyond the estate it would kill the flowers, and then it would be time to pick the sloes; and in here the roses would bloom on.

The silence lengthened. The parson did not know quite how to begin, or even if he *should* begin. Who could say that the dragon might not burn down the whole rose garden, at the suggestion that he might be a sodomite?

The dragon broke the silence. "You love your daughter very much," he said.

This pushed a little too hard at the parson's English reticence. "She is my daughter," he answered.

"Fathers don't always love their children," the dragon said.

There was no emotion in his voice, but he did not look at the parson as he said it, and instead bent to look at moonlight-silvered rose. The parson put his hands in his pockets. His fingers were growing cold. "No," he said. "I suppose not."

He rather expected that the dragon would bring forth some confidence: a stern harsh father, a distant mother more concerned with society than her son, or something of that kind. But instead the dragon said, "I was quite well-liked at Eton, you know."

The parson was puzzled by this turn in the conversation. "Oh?"

"Oh yes," the dragon said eagerly. "The boys used to fight about who should have me come for the holidays. I was an orphan, you see, so there was no reason for me to come home. I could ride and shoot and come up with games to beguile a rainy day, and at Oxford I led the fellows in punt jousting – with punting poles for the lances, and heralds announcing the challengers, and everyone going over into the water at the end. 'Briars is always good for a lark' – that's what they said. They called me Briars."

An image rose before the parson, indistinct and yet compelling, of undergraduates on the banks of the Isis cheering the spectacle, and the two boats clumsily nosing at each other, and the dragon at the center of it all – not a dragon but a laughing young man. Thoughtless perhaps, full of himself doubtless – what undergraduate was not? But young and well-liked and alive, and not at all the bitter goblin that a hundred years of near-solitude had made him.

It struck the parson that it had been quite foolish of the enchantress to try to force the young man to learn to love by cutting him off almost entirely from human contact.

I'm sorry, he wanted to say – which was not the right response at all. He fumbled for words, and he said, "Briars? What was it short for?"

"Briarley," the dragon said. His head jerked back

sharply, as if he had been struck by a sudden realization, and he said, "Allow me to introduce myself. My name is Ambrose Briarley."

There was a brief pause, and then the parson realized that there was an obvious corollary, and that it would not be kind to force to dragon to ask a thing that he ought by any code of politeness to have asked weeks ago. "My name is Harper," the parson said. "Edward Harper."

He held out his hand to shake. The dragon stared at it for a very long moment, and then all his manners seemed to come rushing back to him; he took the parson's hand and shook it gingerly as if he were afraid he might shake the parson's arm off. His palm was warm and dry, and his claws, sharp as they looked, did not scratch the parson's skin.

"Pleased to meet you," the parson said; and the dragon bowed over his hand, in the old courtly style.

And, although the parson had not managed to ask his question – yet he went to bed that night with the feeling that he had made good progress, nonetheless.

CHAPTER 13

The parson dreamed of Rupert Spiles that night –
Rupert Spiles walking hand in hand with the
parson's own dear wife Emily, which was very odd,
as they had never met in life. They walked in a
glade in a woodland, with the sunshine pouring
down on their fair hair, so that they glowed golden
in the sun.

The parson stood in the shadows at the edge of
the wood, and watched. Emily wore the rose tea
dress she had loved so much that she wore it years
after it had fallen out of fashion; and Rupert walked
in his shirtsleeves, with his sleeves rolled up to the
elbows, as if he were about to pole a punt down the
Isis.

The parson could not call out to them, did not try
to call out to them. He watched them walk together,
though they never seemed to get farther away; and
talk together, although the parson could not hear
them; and time seemed to stretch like honey.

They turned back to look at him. They were both

so young, impossibly young in the sunlight; and Emily held out her hand.

And then the sound of barking awakened the parson. He lay in bed, disquieted – for it is always disquieting to dream that your dead are beckoning to you – and yet in some strange way decided.

He must speak to the dragon about his suspicions, after all, even if it did make the dragon flame. Only light could heal shame.

The barking continued. It was Daisy, he thought, barking in the hall. Not barking as a guard dog might bark, but barking with supreme happiness.

There was another sound too, at once very odd and yet familiar. The parson sat up slowly – today he would pay the price for all that walking yesterday, he could tell – listening, listening.

Roller skates. That was what it sounded like. When Rose was eight, she had received a pair of roller skates for Christmas, and skated up and down the flagged floors of the parsonage all winter. They had rattled very much like that.

The parson was so fascinated that he paused only to throw on his dressing gown before he went to peek out the bedroom door. The sound had grown far distant, and he could not at first see anyone – and indeed, if Annie or Hugh had a pair of roller skates, perhaps he would not see anything – but then the sound grew louder again, and louder and louder, and still the parson saw no one, but then he chanced to glance down.

And there was Daisy, with what appeared to be half of a roller skate attached to her hindquarters, propelling herself down the hall with her good front legs. Her tongue lolled joyfully out of her mouth.

She gave a rather breathless bark at the sight of the parson. Instantly she diverted from her course and dashed at him full tilt – only it transpired that she had not yet mastered the art of stopping, and tried to come to a halt far too late, and connected with his shin with a solid thwack.

The parson gave an involuntary shout and grabbed the doorjamb.

"Daisy!" the dragon boomed. The dog pressed herself against the parson's leg as the dragon stormed down the hall, his wings brushing the walls and knocking the paintings askew as he came. "I'm sorry. Blasted dog! Did she hurt you?"

"Not as such, no," wheezed the parson, who felt rather as if his leg might split beneath him. "Are you responsible for this..." He waved his hand at Daisy, whose tail wagged cautiously above the attached roller skate. "Creation?"

"No," the dragon said, wings ruffling, head lowering, and the parson had the sudden impression that the dragon felt quite as shy as Daisy.

"I think it's rather splendid," the parson assured him, as heartily as he could. "Only she'll have to work on stopping, won't she?"

"She already went down a staircase today," the dragon said glumly.

"Well, her spirits are unharmed, at least," the parson commented, and knelt clumsily to ruffle the little dog's ears. Daisy licked his hand with enthusiasm, her tail wagging so wildly that the roller skated skidded on the floor. "Wherever did you get a roller skate?"

"We ordered it from Harrods," said the dragon.

"*Harrods*!" The incongruity startled the parson.

The dragon seemed to mistake the source of that surprise. "I am not so entirely ungenerous as you seem to think me," he said.

"Indeed and he buys us Christmas presents every year," Annie said.

The parson gave a start of surprise, and backed more carefully behind the door, so the girl would not see his bare legs. "Oh, sorry," Annie said. "Me and Hugh came along to see the fun. I suppose we should've said we were here, only we forget, you know, because it's been so long since we've had any visitors and anyhow the master can see us…"

"Can he?" The parson was fascinated. "Do you use a sort of sonar?" he asked the dragon, and realized as he said it that they very likely had never heard of sonar here.

But before he could reframe the question, the dragon answered it. "I can see heat," he said, his voice so flinty that the parson did not pursue the subject, even though questions flocked like crows in his mind.

"A few years ago I asked the master for a pair of roller skates," Annie explained, and the parson's mind snapped back to the subject at hand. "Only the strap broke on one of the skates, so he had to get me another pair – and just the other day I was thinking about poor Daisy and those old broken skates came into my head, and I said, 'Hugh, don't you think we could make my old skates into a sort of bath chair for Daisy?'"

"Only it's better than a bath chair," Hugh said,

and there was a touch of pride in his voice, "because she can push it herself, can't she?"

"One thinks that perhaps the human species might have done better not to have evolved bipedality," the parson observed lightly. But his little joke met a blank stare from the dragon and puzzled silence from Annie and Hugh. He recalled that Darwin's theory of evolution must be quite alien to them. Indeed, Darwin himself might not have thought of it yet in 1840.

"I daresay God knew what he was doing," Annie said at last. "We'd be in a poor way without hands, wouldn't we?"

"Yes, of course," the parson said. "I was only thinking that a four-legged creature who loses a leg is often only slightly hindered by it; whereas for a man, the loss of any one limb may be a disaster, because we have only two of each."

Another pause greeted this observation. Then the dragon cleared his throat, and scratched the back of his neck beneath the frill, and said, "I have decided to give you Uncle Roderick's cane to keep. The ivory-handled one that you like so well."

The parson was a little annoyed – he had not really meant to reference his own occasional lameness – but also, almost against his will, rather touched. "I would not like to take a family heirloom."

"Oh, it is no matter. It is not as if there will be heirs to…"

"Loom it?" the parson said, smiling at this ludicrous play off the word *heirloom*; and somehow that made everything easier. "Thank you," he said.

"It is a beautiful piece of workmanship. Did your uncle bring it from India?"

"Oh yes," the dragon said. "He told the most marvelous stories of the place, and when I was a child I always wanted to go." A great gloom seemed to grow upon him. "One might imagine that a creature with wings could roam hither and yon on this earth, but indeed I am chained to this place. I can fly where I will, but I seem repelled by the very ground if I try to land anywhere else: it is like trying to force two magnets together at their south poles…"

The parson decided that he had better distract the dragon before he really got going on this self-pitying line of thought. "I shall get dressed," the parson said, "and then I think we ought to take Daisy down to the garden."

Daisy found, even as Rose had found as a child, that the grass offered an unpleasant impediment for roller skate wheels. She grew bogged down, and soon abandoned the attempt, raising her soft brown eyes piteously to the dragon and giving a wee sad bark, as if to say, "Pick me up."

The dragon's purported heart of stone was not proof against the sound. He scooped the dog up into his arms, and fondled her soft falling ears with a hand.

"Oh, do let's take her in the ballroom," Annie suggested. "There's ever so much space there. And Mrs. Price is making a syllabub, and we could all have it together, like we was at a ball ourselves – couldn't we?"

"Mrs. Price'll say you're getting above yourself,"

Hugh said.

"Well, let her! If I've got less than two months to go on living, I'd like to live a bit, wouldn't you?"

The parson glanced at the dragon. His long face remained impassive, but his hand paused on Daisy's head. The dog turned and butted her nose against his palm.

"All right," the dragon said. "Let us go to the ballroom, then."

The parson had envisioned a ballroom such as one might see in a motion picture: a vast soaring ceiling and a crystal chandelier. But this was a country ballroom, designed for the comfortable landed gentry, the sort of place where the characters in an Austen novel might have danced: large and spacious certainly, but cavernous no.

The vast smooth floor sent Daisy nearly mad with delight. She careened about on her half-skate, yipping, her stub of a tail streaming out behind her. She collided with the walls and shook herself off and then raced off in another direction; and they all sat and watched and laughed, and indeed began to clap when Daisy managed to turn herself early enough to skim past the wall instead of banging into it.

"Unnatural thing," Mrs. Price announced, but almost fondly, when she came into the room bearing a great floating punchbowl that must have been a syllabub. The syllabub of 1840 seemed a very different beast than that of 1939 – 1940 having no syllabub to speak of, on account of rationing.

"Oh, Daisy's darling, Mrs. Price," Annie said. "Do sit and watch and maybe you'll love her as much as we do. Maybe if we *all* love her, that's what we need to break the curse."

"Never held with giving a dog the same name as you might give to a person," Mrs. Price said.

But nonetheless a chair pulled out, and the upholstery on the seat compressed, and they all sat round the table and drank syllabub and watched Daisy, and had a jolly time.

Daisy grew tired eventually, and the dragon lifted her onto his lap and unstrapped the roller skate, at which point she curled up and fell asleep; which became his excuse not to dance when Annie asked him, after Hugh had fetched his guitar – "Another Christmas present," Annie explained to the parson, as if jealous to display the dragon's generosity.

And so the parson danced with Annie, and Mrs. Price too, and found to his amusement that the mental pictures he had built of them were not quite right: for Annie was no slip of a girl, but a tall Amazon of a lass, and Mrs. Price not a comfortably fat cook but a woman so skinny that the parson scarcely felt it when she stepped on his feet.

The parson's leg did not allow for a great deal of dancing. But afterward they spent the long afternoon around the table, and the parson learned the words to Hugh's old Scottish ballads, until the late afternoon sun slanted in through the tall windows and cast long golden rectangles of light on the floor. Then Hugh declared his fingers too sore to play anymore.

Then Mrs. Price and Annie bore him off to put witch hazel on his fingers, and that left the parson and the dragon alone in the ballroom, with Daisy still asleep on the dragon's lap, and the dragon slowly, slowly stroking her soft ears.

There was a golden peace about the moment, which made it seem as though nothing could go very wrong. And so the parson said, almost idly, "I have been thinking more about this curse of yours."

"Oh?" The dragon did not sound very interested.

"Miss Clarence suggested to me that I have erred," the parson said. "She thinks that I have been giving too much pride of place to abstract ideas about the nature of love, and not considering the character of a woman who would lay such a disproportionate curse."

"Perhaps it is simply unbreakable." The dragon did not sound surprised, and it struck the parson that he had all but given up decades ago.

"No," said the parson, after some hesitation. "I have little direct experience with magic, you understand, but in stories it always seems that curses are breakable if you just know how to go about it."

"So you think it is romantic, after all. All this folderol about dogs was useless, just as I thought." The dragon made to push Daisy off his lap. Daisy looked up at him and whined, and he rested a heavy hand on her head instead.

The parson grew exasperated. "It's not real love if it is only a means to an end," he said.

But the dragon ignored him. He set Daisy aside and stood up, pacing, his hands clasped behind his back and his wings rustling with agitation. "Of course you are telling me this now that your daughter is gone," he said bitterly.

"Would she have made any difference?" the parson asked. "Is it possible for you to love a woman?"

The dragon froze. He understood: the parson saw that in the rigid line of his back, his half-spread wings, the choked note in his voice as he said, "What are you saying to me?"

And the parson awakened then to the fact that he was treading on dangerous ground: but it was too late for retreat. "Please," he said, "I don't mean to insult you. It is only that we must be working from a basis of truth if we are to have any hope of breaking this curse."

The dragon whipped round. He stalked toward the parson like an angry tiger. Daisy began to bark.

"You don't mean to insult me," the dragon said, his voice low and trembling with rage, but rising to a shout as he continued. "You don't mean to insult me, but you call me a sodomite! By God, what do you call an insult, then?"

"I didn't – " the parson began.

"Don't mince words with me! God, I hate clergymen. Mealy-mouthed and dirty-minded, seeing beastliness in every corner! How dare you, how dare you, I have fed you and sheltered you under my own roof, how *dare* you accuse me!"

Daisy barked and barked. The dragon thrust back his head and fountained fire toward the high ceiling. He flew upward, winging round the room in a great uneven oval, releasing gouts of fire so that the sparks rained down. The parson took off his wool jacket and slung it over Daisy, to protect her fur from the sparks. The little dog trembled and barked.

One of the tapestries caught fire near the top. The dragon gave a trumpeting scream and flew at it, beating at it with his wings and his bare clawed scaly feet, until the tapestry broke in two and the lower portion fell down in a smoldering heap; and then the dragon swung round, and the parson ducked even though the dragon was on the other side of the room.

He did not see the dragon break through the window. He only heard the shattering sound of the glass, and saw the broken pieces glittering in the sunset, and the dragon's dark shape against the golden sky as he flew away.

"Well," the parson said. His knees trembled, and he knelt, only mostly on purpose, to put a soothing hand on the dog. "That went well, Daisy, did it not?"

The dog only shivered in reply.

The parson began to laugh unsteadily, although it offered little relief to his nerves. For he knew that it was all to do again. The dragon's swift apprehension and his rage had not been that of a man falsely accused, but the bitter terror of a man who believes that his darkest secret has been found out.

CHAPTER 14

The dragon disappeared.

He must still be on the grounds: he had said that he could not land anywhere else. But he stopped coming down for breakfast or for dinner.

"Brooding in his tower most like," Mrs. Price advised, as she put a cutlet in Daisy's bowl. The dog nibbled at it listlessly, then rested her nose against her paws, and gazed at the parson with pitiful brown eyes. "He gets like that betimes. Don't fret on it."

"Perhaps I should climb his tower to speak to him?" the parson suggested. He rested a hand on Daisy's soft ears. She sniffed at his palm and then dropped her head again. "I might tell him his dog misses him."

"Oh, better not," Annie said. "I climbed his tower once and he threw a boot at my head. There's naught to do but wait it out."

"But there are less than two months to break the curse," the parson objected.

A heavy sigh answered him. He could not tell if

it came from Annie or Mrs. Price.

The parson had a fine hot temper of his own, and it roused up against the dragon now. The parson could understand the violence of the dragon's first reaction, but not this ongoing disregard for Daisy: even if the dragon felt no sense of responsibility for her, still the dog was his best last hope, and it disgusted the parson to see him giving up.

God perhaps could save a sinner against his will. The parson was a mere mortal and laid claim to no such powers.

On the third day the parson took out his bicycle and rode to Briarfield. He told Mrs. Price that he meant to stop at the post office, for he had some idea that any letters from Rose might come to rest there, and never reach the estate; but his temper rose as he rode through the fine bright day, and he thought he might simply ride on to Lesser Innsley. He would put out of his mind forever the dragon and the enchanted house and the poor helpless servants –

Oh, but they would haunt him forever if he did. He drew to an abrupt halt before the little post office, with its sides covered in ivy that had blushed autumn-red, and his thoughts jerked to a halt as well, and he paused to catch his breath. No, he could not leave. He had made himself responsible. He must see the damn thing through.

He tried to cheer himself up in telling the postmistress about Daisy's good health, and the roller skate – "I can't believe we never thought of that!" the postmistress marveled.

But eventually the postmistress gave a start, and

clapped a hand over herself. "I've got a letter for you," she said. "I can't think how I forgot to send it on." Her small eyes bulged behind her thick glasses, and the parson – irritated at the world and thus irritated enough to smack her – assured her that it was quite all right.

He took Rose's letter outside and read it beneath the gold-tipped trees.

To my right worshipful father, may this be delivered in haste –

The parson's lips twitched into a smile. His foul temper fell quite suddenly away. Rose had picked up that ornate old-fashioned habit of salutation when she read the Paston letters at Oxford, and it had become a little joke between them.

She gave him the latest news – insofar as it was possible to tell him anything when she could not say where she was, or what she was doing, or anything else that might impede the war effort. She and a friend had gone on a bicycle ride, *along the seaside or up in the hills or perhaps in the fens – that covers all the possibilities, doesn't it, in case this falls into German hands? You shall simply have to take my word for it that the scenery, whatever it may have been, was lovely. And we saw a most gorgeous sunset, the sky splashed with scarlet and orange.*

The butter turned out to be fairy gold, I'm afraid. Too bad! Too bad!

Yr. right loving & obedient daughter,
Rose

The parson set the letter aside, still smiling, and shaking his head: it had been too much to hope that enchanted food might last beyond the walls of the castle.

He felt stronger now, and calmer, and he folded the letter carefully into the pocket of his waistcoat before he mounted his bicycle again, and turned it back toward the castle. He would go back: he would go back. He would climb the tower steps, and apologize to the dragon.

***

The parson was barely more than halfway up the spiral stair when Daisy began to wriggle and bark in his arms. He held the struggling dog with difficulty. "You might come take her out of my hands!" he called up the stairs.

At first there was no answer, and he began to wonder if the dragon might be elsewhere; and then the dragon bellowed, "I never *asked* you to meddle!"

Daisy barked and barked, and nearly succeeded in wrenching herself from the parson's arms. The parson hoped the dragon would not take the opportunity to fly away out of the windows.

But when the parson at last gained the top of the stairs, he found that the dragon had not moved. The round tower room had wide airy windows and deep windowsills, and views that stretched past the rose garden and the walls of the estate, to the autumn trees beyond.

But the dragon sat with his back to all that, his shoulders stiff, his wings curled about him like a blanket, and his eyes fixed on the portrait of a handsome young man with golden hair and fair strong brows and ludicrous fluffy sideburns that must have been the height of fashion in 1840.

"Go away," the dragon said.

Daisy let out a mournful howl, as if she had understood the words. The parson fondled her ears. "I'm sorry," he said.

The dragon glanced at him. The parson took the opportunity to deposit Daisy in the dragon's lap. The dog put her paws on the dragon's stomach and gazed up in his face.

That gaze might have melted a heart of stone, such as the dragon claimed to have. The dragon rested a hand on top of Daisy's head, and scowled at the parson. "*Now* go away," he said.

"I have come to apologize," the parson said.

"Well," said the dragon, "you've apologized. Now go."

The parson planted his feet. "I have come also," he said, "to tell you a story."

The dragon twisted round, his neck frill flared all about his head. "I have told you I hate parables," the dragon said.

"Not a parable," the parson said. "Only a story. One that makes me look rather shabby."

The dragon snorted. Curls of smoke rose from his nose. Daisy snuffled her nose in his palm.

But he did not tell the parson to go, so the parson seated himself on one of the wide windowsills (the dragon occupied the only seat), and laced his fingers together, and tried to begin.

He failed. "That portrait," the parson said. "Is that how you looked before the curse?"

Now the dragon turned to glare. "Do you think it is some strange man whose picture I keep to inflame my unclean lusts?"

"No," said the parson, and forbore to reference Narcissus. "The servants told me that it was your own portrait that you keep up here."

The dragon shrugged – a movement that lifted his wings, making them ruffle and rearrange themselves. "Yes," he said shortly.

He said no more. The parson looked at the portrait again, contemplating the handsome young man at the height of his youth, and remembered suddenly a young man he had known at Oxford, Cyril Saunders. There was no similarity in appearance: Saunders had been dark and brooding and Byronically handsome – until the gas ate his face at Ypres. Saunders had shot himself after the war.

The Narcissus comparison no longer struck the parson as funny, but sad. He was struggling to find some way to express it when the dragon broke the silence.

"Just go," he said. He tried to rise from his seat, but Daisy began to bark, and he fell back again. "I can see you can't bear to speak to me," he said. "You only stayed at Briarley because of duty in the first place, and that is why you are here now, because you think it is your *duty* to try to win sinners to the light. But it is impossible. You were quite right: quite right; is that what you want to hear? I am a sodomite. Now go!"

The parson did not move. Daisy hunkered down in the dragon's lap.

"Despised," the dragon elaborated, "in the eyes of God. Mrs. Price has the right of it: that beggar woman was no enchantress, but an angel sent to smite me. The curse has been unbreakable from the first."

The dragon fell silent, and again the parson struggled to speak. It was not that he had nothing to say, but too many things. He had felt those selfsame emotions in his youth, that bitterness and burning rage and self-condemnation. In that moment he felt also something he had never expected to feel: and that was a profound compassion for the dragon.

"Briarley," the parson said. The dragon did not look at him. The parson stepped forward and took the dragon's hand in both his own, and then the dragon's head snapped round, so the parson had a brief view of those brown human eyes in the dragon's scaly face.

Then the dragon looked away again. The parson held onto his hand. "Briarley," he said. "I do not come to condemn you. If I could not stand to share a room with you, I could not be alone with myself either: I speak to you as a fellow sinner."

The dragon pulled his hand away. He might have flown were it not for Daisy on his lap. "Don't give me that pap! Fellow sinners, indeed. Just because we are all sinners in the eyes of God – "

"I am not talking about that Calvinist notion of total depravity," the parson interrupted. And, though he loathed the word, he said, "I am speaking to you as a fellow sodomite."

The dragon's mouth fell open. The parson had an unpleasant view of his sharp, shark-like rows of teeth.

Then the dragon's mouth snapped shut again. Two little curls of smoke snorted from his nose. "Impossible," he said.

"Not so. Do you think I would lie to you about such a thing?"

"But," the dragon said. "You are a good man. You have a *daughter*. You must have had a wife."

"Indeed I did," the parson said, "and I loved her very much. But there are men who can love both men and women, as well as men who love only women or men; there was an ancient Greek play, I believe – "

The dragon waved that away with a slash of his hand. "The ancients were a bunch of foul degenerates."

"Not always," the parson said, and then continued eagerly, for this connected to a pet theory. "Although of course sometimes they were. You see, I believe that Paul – "

"Paul!" And the dragon turned away again, disdainful. "Spare me your sermons."

The parson fell silent again. The ancient Greeks – the Bible – these would have brought the conversation to a comfortably abstract ground. The dragon had one hand on Daisy's back, and Daisy's tail wagged very slowly, and she gazed at the parson over the sleeve of the dragon's coat.

"Let us set aside Paul," said the parson. "Let us set aside the Greeks, let us set aside all sermons, let me speak to you not as a man in a pulpit, but as your equal, standing side by side on solid ground. Indeed that is how I should have spoken to you from the beginning, rather than scoffing down at you, and prescribing like a doctor from on high. All my suggestions have been born of my own experience. Even the dog I suggested because a pet dog was a great help to me, after I was discharged from the army and felt that all happiness had drained out of the world for me, because I was a cripple and my beloved friend was dead."

The dragon did not answer for some time: so long in fact that the parson was overcome by doubt, and felt ashamed to have revealed so much, and would have left the room like a whipped dog, except the dragon said, "I do not blame you. After how I treated you the first time we met…" His voice faded out.

"The kidnapping?" the parson said. "The threat to throw me off the roof?"

The dragon ducked his head. "Yes," he said. "After that. You did not owe me any kindness, any sympathy after that: it was more that I deserved even for you to sermonize me from on high."

The parson sat again. Daisy took the dragon's cuff in her ivory teeth, and tugged playfully.

"It is not a matter of deserving," the parson said. He sought for an explanation that the dragon might understand, and could find none, because he was not sure he understood himself. "I stayed because I wanted to help," he said at last. "And I could have helped more if I had judged less. 'There is none righteous, not, not one.'"

110

"You are one of the righteous," the dragon said.

The fervency in his voice embarrassed the parson. He shook his head and stood up and went to the window, and stood with his hands clasped behind his back, gazing beyond the roses and the walls to the golden world of autumn, beyond.

"You are," the dragon insisted. "Do you not believe it? Do you think your sodomy has damned you? You are the first truly good man that I have ever met."

The parson saw that the theological point was perhaps beyond the dragon, and would only confuse him. So he said, "I do not think I am damned. If there are unforgivable sins, they are the sins that the Nazis are committing, and not the fumblings of lustful young men."

"And the church?" the dragon said. There was a suppressed excitement in his voice. "Is this the opinion of the church?"

The parson sighed. "No."

"Of course not," the dragon said. "Because of Leviticus, and Paul. 'God also gave them up to uncleanness through the lusts of their own hearts, to dishonor their own bodies between themselves...'"

Naturally the dragon knew the relevant passage. Certainly it had burned itself in the parson's own brain when he was a young man.

"I have given this great thought," the parson said, speaking slowly, for although he had indeed given it thought, it had been a very long time since he had discussed it with anyone. "I discussed it at some length with my great friend Rupert Spiles. We thought perhaps it was the brutality of the Roman world – the degeneracy of which you spoke – that made Paul write so. Perhaps men used each other so brutally then that he could not conceive of any relation between men that was patient, and kind, and partook of all those other qualities in his great discourse upon love: and yet his words have wrought such a change in our society that even men can love each other now, as they could not in Paul's own time."

The dragon's neck frill rose. "That is sophistry," he broke in. "You made that up to excuse your own sin to yourselves."

"It is possible," the parson agreed. "Certainly that would be the opinion of the church. But…"

"Enough!" The dragon's wings ruffled with agitation. "You may have all your pretty words about it, but in the end it's vile – it's beastly – it's a trap set by the devil to snare men in the dark. You say love is not love if it is a means to an end? But men *always* treat each other as a means to an end, and cast each other aside when that end is met, and never mind about your Davids and Jonathans!"

"You have been treated badly," the parson said gently, "if that is the only relation between men that you have seen."

"I suppose Rupert Spiles never used you so?" The dragon's voice was scathing.

"No."

"Then he did not live long enough to tire of you."

The words were meant to wound, but they did not. The parson felt such an intensity of compassion for the dragon that he might not have felt himself wounded had the dragon thrown him down the stairs. He could almost feel the dragon's fear, and anger, his yearning to be convinced and his conviction that the arguments might be the snares of the devil. The parson had felt all those things himself.

"What I know," the parson said, "is that it was the love of Rupert Spiles that taught me how to love. And it was not romantic love only, *eros* as the Greeks would call it, that I learned from him – although it was *eros* that opened the door for me: it was the intensity of *eros* that allowed me also to learn of faithful friendship, *philia*, and affection, and even the *agape* love that is Christian charity. All these things began for me in the tenderness I felt for Rupert. I could not have loved my wife Emily, or my daughter Rose, or my parishioners, or indeed loved you, if I had not learned through Rupert Spiles how to fulfill the commandment, and love another as myself."

Another long silence followed. But this time the parson felt no urge to flee. He sat down again, and waited. The dragon's head drooped low, so that the parson could see beneath his scaly neck frill, to the tender human nape of his neck.

After a long time, the dragon said, "And he was your lover?"

"Yes."

"And you loved him with your body – and that did not render the love impure?"

"It did not," the parson said. He had always believed this, but nonetheless in saying it, he felt a weight slide off his shoulders: it had been so long since he had spoken of Rupert Spiles, not merely as a friend but as everything that Rupert had been to him, that their golden happiness had in the darkness become mildewed with shame.

"Perhaps your love for you wife purified it?" the dragon suggested.

"It did not need purifying," the parson said.

The dragon let out a shuddering breath. Then the dragon lifted his head, and stretched out his wings, as a man might stretch his arms after sitting for a very long time; and the parson saw a flash of light through one of the dragon's wings, and realized that it was torn.

"What is the matter with your wing?" the parson asked.

He tried to ask casually, but the dragon bristled anyway, and drew his wings tight again. "It's nothing," the dragon said.

"Admittedly I am but little acquainted with dragon physiology," the parson said, "but it seems unlikely to me that there are meant to be rents in your wings."

The dragon's wings and his neck frill drooped. "I cut it on the glass when…" he said, and his voice drooped away too.

"You flew through the window," the parson supplied, and the dragon gave his long head one sharp downward nod of assent.

"But truly it is nothing," the dragon said. "It will heal itself in a few days. I have suffered such before."

"You make it a habit to fly through windows?" the parson asked.

The dragon half-rose, wings ruffling in irritation,

and Daisy woke with a yip. The dragon sat again. "Don't mock me," he told the parson.

The parson lifted his hands. "I am sorry," he said. "But I have some little experience mending birds' wings – "

"Of course you do," the dragon scoffed.

The parson ignored him. "So will you let me see your wing?"

The dragon ruffled his wings. "All right."

He opened his wings, and they stretched across the round tower room. Indeed, he had to curve them inward to make them fit.

The parson came to stand beside the dragon's shoulder. He could feel the feverish warmth of his body – "Are you always so warm?" he asked the dragon, and reached out to touch a hand to his forehead.

The dragon shied away. "Always," he said tersely. "Fire burns within me."

The parson supposed that indeed it must.

The parson had mended birds' wings often enough. Indeed, he was well known for it: the children of his parish often brought him injured songbirds. But the dragon's wing was not fashioned after the manner of birds, but of bats, with a thick membrane stretched over a framework of bone.

The parson had always thought the dragon's wings black before. But standing so close, with the bright light of the sun through the windows, he could see that they were a very dark green. He wondered whether that greenness spilled onto the skin of the dragon's back, and how far it reached – and reminded himself that he was here for a purpose, and not mere scientific curiosity.

The dragon shivered when the parson rested his hands on the spar of his wing. He drew in a quick unsteady breath.

"Did I hurt you?" the parson asked.

The dragon shook his head. "No."

But his voice still sounded unsteady, and the parson thought it might be mere schoolboy stoicism that held him back.

But it didn't seem to hurt him as the parson moved his hands carefully over the bones of the wing, checking for breaks or sensitive places. The dragon's wings were warm, which should not be surprising: they were a part of his body; of course they should be warm. But they seemed such an unnatural appendage to sprout from a man's back that somehow the parson had expected them to be cool, mechanical.

He checked the joint last, where the wing attached to the dragon's shoulder blade. The dragon wore a frock coat, and a shirt beneath that, and both pieces of clothing had long openings sewn up the back for the wings to come through – which exposed enough skin that the parson could see that the greenness of the wing did indeed spill onto the dragon's back. The color grew less dark, more obviously green than it was on its wing; and it quickly broke up into mere emerald freckles against the dragon's pale skin. The parson wanted to touch one and see if it felt scaly.

But he did not. He felt a sudden rush of vertigo, and stayed were he was, bent over, one hand grasping the dragon's stool and the other pressed against the dragon's upper back, just above the sprouting wing. The dragon's heartbeat drummed against his palm.

The vertigo passed. The parson removed his hands. "The bones seem well enough," he said.

"I could have told you as much." The dragon's voice was low.

The parson stepped back, unsteady, and bent to peer at the rent in the wing. The wing was simply a thin stretched layer of skin, like the canvas of an aeroplane – although unlike canvas, this seemed to be knitting itself back together. The ends of the rent were already closing up, held together by a thin delicate layer of skin that was almost translucent as yet.

The parson did not touch it. Indeed, as the dragon had said, there did not seem to be much that he could do.

He stood too quickly, which made him a little dizzy, so that he was unsteady as he stepped away from the dragon. His hands felt dry, and strange, and he clasped them behind his back. "It seems you were quite right," he admitted. "Forgive me. I hoped there was something I could do to help."

"You're done?" the dragon said, and perhaps there was a touch of disappointment in his voice. He folded his wings against his back, and said, "I told you it was quite unnecessary to have a look."

The parson inclined his head. "Does it pain you?" he asked. "Is that why we have seen so little of you these past days?"

The dragon turned his head away. "No."

He had indeed been sulking. "Then you can

rejoin us?" the parson asked. "I have missed you."

The dragon's head turned sharply toward him, and then dropped away again. "You're lying."

"I am not." And the parson realized, with some irritation, that he was indeed telling the truth. "You are intensely irritating," he told the dragon, "but nonetheless, it seems that I get bored when you are gone."

The dragon's long scaled snout was not made for smiling, but nonetheless there seemed something of a smile in the way he stood up, and the jaunty set of his wings. "It is only that you're missing your village," he said stubbornly. "You're used to having care of all the lost souls there. I am only a substitute."

"Good God, Briarley!" the parson said, and controlled himself. Indeed in his own village he had parishioners with that same self-torturing tendency to insist that any kind thing that anyone might say or do for them was mere politeness. It did no good, he had found, to argue with them directly.

"Daisy," the parson said instead, "has certainly missed you."

The dragon looked at the dog on his lap. "What's the use? Now that we know the curse must be broken through romantic love – "

"We do not *know* any such thing," the parson said. "And even if Daisy is no use to you, you are certainly of use to her. She's barely eating her cutlets. If you put her in her roller skate she drags herself about the house sniffing for traces of you. It's pitiful."

Daisy, ever helpful, bit the dragon's cuff and

tugged playfully at his sleeve.

The dragon removed her teeth from his clothing. Daisy nibbled at his claw instead. "It will only make her sadder," the dragon said stubbornly, "when the curse ends, and I'm turned into a pillar of salt. It would be better for her – "

"It would be better for her," the parson interrupted, "if you will refrain from giving up, just yet. All of us are going to die one day, but that is no reason to fling ourselves off the parapet right now."

The dragon snorted.

"Daisy already loves you," the parson added. "You can see that very well. One half of the curse is already broken. Could you not bring her downstairs and strap her back into her roller skate and see if you might find it within yourself to love her back?"

He went to stand at the head of the stairs, and looked back at the dragon, expectant. The dragon sighed, and ruffled his wings, and made a great to-do about picking up Daisy. He picked up her skate by the straps, at which point Daisy's tail stub began to whip back and forth, and she began to bark.

The dragon lifted her closer to him, and growled at her, "I am only doing this because it amuses me, you know."

Daisy licked his snout.

CHAPTER 15

"Why did you become a parson?" the dragon asked.

It had been three days since their conversation in the tower. The dragon had returned to the regular activities of the house, and the parson to his habit of joining the dragon in the garden when he had the chance, although the air grew colder every day.

It was late afternoon when the dragon asked his question. The shadows were long, and they had been walking quietly in the grass, with Daisy trundling along behind in her roller skate, and no sound but the occasional squeak of her wheels.

"I wanted to help people," the parson said. "And I had seen enough of blood in the war, so I did not want to be a doctor; and in any case a doctor must worry about whether his patients can pay. A parson is paid by his parish to help everyone."

"To help everyone," the dragon echoed, as if this were an entirely novel take on the purpose of churchmen.

Indeed, perhaps it was to him, the parson

thought. In 1840, the church had been one of the few positions open to gentlemen, and attractive because it was a sinecure. Many pulpits must inevitably have been filled by men with no vocation.

"You simply don't seem like a churchman at all," the dragon said.

"Oh, I don't agree with that," the parson said easily. "I am dreadfully prone to sermonizing, as you may have noticed. And very fond of a parable."

"Yes, but you aren't the least bit canting or hypocritical," the dragon said.

The parson's mouth worked – he attempted valiantly to suppress a smile – but his amusement exploded out of him in a snort.

The dragon seemed to realize that perhaps he had been rude. "I didn't mean," he said, and stopped short, realizing perhaps that there was no uninsulting thing such a statement could have meant.

"Oh, don't worry about it." The parson waved it away with a hand. "I long ago ceased to pay any attention to the prattling of the landed gentry. They are entirely too full of themselves – "

"Now wait – " the dragon began, his wings flapping in indignation. The parson once again failed to suppress a snort. "Oh! You are... joking?" the dragon said.

"More or less," the parson said. "More or less."

They had reached a clearing among the roses that contained an unfamiliar birdbath. Daisy creaked over to it, sniffing around the base, and then did her duty by this strange new boundary marker.

"I only meant," the dragon said, "that most of the churchmen I've known have been dreadful hypocrites about that sort of thing: tipplers who preach about temperance, and adulterers who rail against the lusts of the flesh, and all that. The chaplains at school lectured us about idleness, but never worked themselves."

"I suppose a tippler may know the evils of drink more nearly than a man who never drinks to excess," the parson said mildly. "But your point is taken: it is a great pity in my view that we expect perfection of our preachers, and have made it impossible for them to acknowledge their own struggles, when in truth it is our struggles – our weaknesses – that draw together all of humanity. If you want someone to guide you through a labyrinth, you must choose someone who has been there before."

The dragon opened his mouth, as if to agree, and then closed it again and knit his brow, apparently trying to work out whether the parson agreed with him or not. At length he said – "Do you think sodomy is a labyrinth that you escaped?"

The parson was startled. The topic had been utterly dropped between them since they had spoken of it in the dragon's tower, and he had not expected the dragon to bring it back up. "No," he said, rather stiffly, for he knew that he was at odds with church doctrine on this point. "My beloved friend died. Perhaps if he had lived I would have remained happily ensnared all my life."

"Then you think it *is* a snare."

The parson bent, and plucked a grass stem from

the ground, and tore off all the seeds. "No," he said, more stiffly still. "But you must understand I am speaking only as myself in this – I am utterly at sea – I might be leading you quite astray. The church certainly does not agree."

"But that's just it!" the dragon trumpeted, his wings lifting in his excitement. "How could you join the church that condemns you?"

"As if the British Isles overflowed with professions that welcomed homosexuality," the parson scoffed.

"Homo…" The dragon's voice trailed off in the thicket of unfamiliar syllables.

"Sexual relations between two men," the parson said. "Or two women. It is said to be common in the theater, but even there people dare not be *open* – and in any case I have no talent as an actor, whereas the good Lord has seen fit to give me some talent for giving sermons and sitting with the sick."

The dragon contemplated this. His neck frill drooped. "I had hoped," he admitted, "that what you said to me – in the tower – that it reflected some sea change in society."

"I'm afraid not. I am not alone in my views, but we are far from a majority, believe me."

Daisy rubbed herself against the dragon's leg. The dragon lifted her in his arms, and she licked his scaly face.

They had been standing still for some time, and the parson's leg had grown stiff. The birdbath was empty, and he perched on the edge, with his stick in the ground to give him balance as he rested his leg. "I am eminently suited to my profession in every other way," he said. "And in truth I feel that my own experiences have given me a clearer view of temptation – and the difference between what society calls sin, and what must be right and wrong in the eyes of God. And in any case…" He twisted his stick in the ground, drilling a hole in the earth. "Once I met Emily, I believed I had grown out of…" He paused, and his lips quirked. "My youthful follies."

"Had you?"

The parson shrugged.

"*Had* you?" the dragon insisted.

"I found that it was not so true as I had hoped." The parson shrugged again. "But if you are hoping for a sordid tale of tumbling with the curate in the sacristy, I have no such stories to tell. I have been true to Emily and to Rupert since they died."

He expected some reaction from the dragon: perhaps shock at that blasphemous suggestion. But the dragon fell silent, stroking Daisy's head, although he seemed almost unconscious of the dog's stub of a tail whipping ecstatically back and forth.

"Tell me about him," the dragon said.

"About who?" said the parson.

It was an honest question, but the dragon's frill ruffled, as if he thought the parson were being deliberately dense. "About Rupert Spiles."

"What about him?" the parson asked. There was a touch of chill to his voice, which he had not intended; but he felt in that moment rather like a knight who has been asked to gossip about his lady.

"Oh, I don't know," the dragon said. He clicked

his clawed thumbs together. "What did he look like?"

The parson's hackles smoothed: that seemed innocent enough. But it took him some time to compose an answer. After Rupert died, the parson had locked him away in a box in the back of his mind, like a picture that might fade with too much exposure to light – only to discover that memories, unlike pictures, fade even faster in the darkness.

So it took some time for him to alight on the memory, and when he did it stung him, and he had to catch his breath. "He was tall," said the parson, "and thin, and golden-haired. He played cricket – not well enough to make the eleven – but well enough to play on the county team, the summer I went out to visit him at his place…"

The warm memory seemed to overlay the chilly day. Rupert Spiles, like a statue in chryselephantine, standing gold and ivory in the sunlight with his shining hair and cricket whites – standing over a young Edward Harper, who was not a parson yet but only a student at Oxford, lying propped on his elbows in the grass and laughing, because it was the summer of 1914 and they were young and would live forever.

"Do you miss him?" the dragon asked.

"What do you think?" the parson asked, peevish.

"I am sorry."

The dragon's voice was soft, and then the parson was sorry for his own snappishness. "The edge has gone off it," the parson said. "But yes. I think that if one truly loves someone, then one does not ever entirely cease to miss that person."

A silence fell between them after. The cold of the birdbath had penetrated the parson's trousers, and now his seat was cold. He stood up, and lurched on his bad leg – it got worse in the chill – and caught his balance again, and decided it was time to head back for the house.

The dragon fell in step beside him. He had tucked Daisy beneath his coat, and she peeked out at the parson, panting happily.

"I am sorry I snapped at you, Briarley," the parson said. "You caught me on a hurt place, as you see."

"I am sorry too," the dragon said. "It was like prodding a bruise – when I should have known it would hurt you."

"Well, now you will know next time," the parson said. "And do better. That is the best that any of us can do."

They had been walking in the garden for some time, and should have been deep in the maze. But they came very quickly to the edge of the rose hedges, and found themselves on the thin strip of lawn below the house, looking in the window of the library. A book lay open on a table, and as the parson looked, a page turned. Annie must be reading.

"I wish you would call me Briars," the dragon said suddenly.

The parson turned to look at him. "What's wrong with Briarley?"

"My schoolmates called me Briars," the dragon said.

"We didn't go to school together," the parson

objected.

"My schoolmates are all dead," the dragon said, and now he was the one to sound peevish. "And they did not miss *me*. We would not be here if any one of them had."

"Do you think it would have broken the curse?" the parson asked. "I know it saved the servants, but after all, they were not the focus of the enchantress's ire. If your friends came, might they not have found the gates shut against them?"

Smoke rose from the dragon's nose. "I tell you they did not come!"

"All right," the parson said, and let the subject go. It seemed unlikely to him that no one had tried at all – but it had been a hundred years ago, so what did he know? And schoolboys could be fickle: a boy who was beloved for his larks might be forgotten, once the larks stopped.

It must have embittered the dragon to think that the schoolmates he loved so well had abandoned him.

And the parson thought suddenly that it was time and past time that he thought of the dragon by his name, and not just 'the dragon.' That had been suitable enough when the dragon was a mere kidnapper, but less so now that the dragon was becoming – a friend.

Yes, a friend. Exasperating though the parson often found him, he had grown fond of the man.

The thought hit the parson like a pang in his heart. He would be sorry indeed if the curse ran its course, and the dragon – no, and *Briarley* sank into hell as Mrs. Price expected, or turned into a pillar of salt, or a topiary of roses.

"Briars," the parson said, testing it out, and was pained – both in spirit and in flesh – by the strength with which the dragon gratefully gripped his hand.

"Does that not sound friendlier, Harper?" the dragon (no, *Briarley*) asked.

"Yes," the parson said. And then he said – rather tentatively – half-wishing he could take it back as the words left his lips: "If you wanted – you could call me Teddy."

"Teddy!"

"It is what they called me growing up," the parson said. "My brother, and my friends, before I went away to school." Dead, dead, almost all dead. "No one has called me that since Emily died."

"Teddy." The dragon said it carefully, as if trying it out. "Do you know," he said, "I do not think I could."

The parson, much to his own surprise, felt intensely disappointed. "Oh," he said. "Well. You do not have to, you know. Harper is quite as well."

They crossed the grass. The shadow of the house lay across the lawn, and the air grew quite cold as they passed into the shade.

"I might," the dragon said – they had reached the door now; the dragon opened it, and the parson went through, and stood just inside, waiting. "I might call you Edward?"

And the parson felt a warm glow, which was nothing to do with his entry into the draughty house. (Even magic could not heat an English country house.) "You might," he agreed.

"Edward the Confessor," the dragon said

happily.

The parson might have thrown something at him, if he had anything to hand. Instead he took the handle, and shut the door on the dragon, and hurried away down the hall, using the cane to put extra swing into his step. He caught sight of his reflection in a mirror that hung at the end of the hall, and found that he was smiling.

CHAPTER 16

Time passed. The parson now went up to the dragon's lair every day, to gaze out the windows at the changing trees beyond the walls. Brown and red leaves had utterly replaced green, and in turn were falling to reveal bare black branches. All Hallow's Eve was on its way.

Yet a kind of peace reigned within the estate. The roses bloomed, and the dinner arrived everlastingly the same each night, and it seemed impossible to believe that anything would ever change.

Every day they walked in the rose garden: Briarley with Daisy in his arms, and the parson alongside him. It had grown so cold that a white frost often rimed the scarlet roses in the morning, and the frosted grass crunched under their feet. It had ceased to bother that parson that the frosted roses never withered.

One such morning, with the sun shining impotently against the cold, they found a clearing among the hedges. A fountain stood in the center, with a sculpture of a faun balanced on one hoof, and water trickling from his panpipes into a shallow basin. The parson touched his fingers to the water. "It's warm," he murmured.

Briarley set Daisy down on the lip of the fountain. She bent down her nose to sniff at the water, and drew back when a drop splashed on her nose; and then bent forward, and stuck her nose in, and finding it warm pulled herself into the water, and paddled happily along with her front feet.

The parson smiled. Briarley watched, his face unchanging. His snout did not allow for smiles; but the parson had grown adept at reading his eyes and his forehead, and those were not smiling either.

"Mrs. Price thinks the infernal fires of Hell warm this place," Briarley said. "That is why the grass stays green and the roses grow all year, she thinks."

Well, no wonder. That was not a cheery thought. "I should think the infernal fires of Hell might keep the frost away," the parson said.

But Briarley was not listening. "Harper," he said, and there was a hesitant note in his voice. "I know I have told you to leave many times, and before I have not really meant it, but..."

And now he paused, for so long that the parson said, "My dear Briars, you cannot think I'm going to cut and run at this late date."

"I should like you to go on All Hallow's Eve." Briarley said it all in a rush, and lifted a hand to forestall the parson from speaking. "The ground may open up and swallow this whole house down to Hell for all we know. Indeed that seems very likely.

And I can do nothing…"

Here his voice faltered. The parson reached out and put a hand on his arm. "Steady on," he said.

"I can do nothing for Mrs. Price, or Annie or Hugh," Briarley said. He stared straight ahead, unblinking, and his chest heaved as he spoke. "But I can assure that you are well out of it – and that you will take – take Daisy with you. Get on your bicycle and go to Briarfield."

"It is still two weeks to All Hallow's Eve," the parson said.

"Do you really think anything can change in two weeks?" Briarley asked.

"Everything can change in an instant," the parson said. "The Luftwaffe drops a bomb, and an entire apartment building is wiped out. The lawn mower must have ruined Daisy's legs in moments." The dog barked happily at the sound of her name, and paddled over to them, and Briarley scooped her out of the water.

"For the better," Briarley clarified, tucking Daisy inside his coat to keep her safe from the chill air. "Can things change for the better in two weeks?"

"Romeo and Juliet fell in love in an instant," the parson said.

Smoke rose from the dragon's nostrils. "Most kinds of love," he replied, and it sounded like he was having difficulty controlling his voice, "take longer than that."

This was true. Daisy had been their last ditch effort, and the curse remained unbroken. The parson knew from bitter experience that there came a time when holding out corporeal hope to the sick became a kind of mockery: they would not get well on this earth and they knew it, and they resented being exhorted to have a false hope.

He had seen enough of sickness and of death that he could comfort the dying. But now his whole soul rebelled. Did prison chaplains feel like this, when they went to comfort a condemned man as his execution approached? If they doubted the justness of the sentence, – indeed, when they *knew* the sentence to be unjust – did their office torment them?

"It is unfair," the parson burst out; "it is unfair. What have you done that a thousand other Englishmen would not have done in your place? If it is wicked to turn away a beggar, if we have turned away from the standards of hospitality set forth in the scriptures, why then we are all wicked, and ought to suffer together – even as the people of Sodom and Gomorrah suffered. It was the failure of their hospitality that was their true sin; and indeed, we are all Sodomites, all across Europe our hospitality has failed. We turn the stranger from our gates and spit on the strangers already inside, and why should you be cursed for it when the rest of us continue in our sinful ways?"

Briarley gazed at him, astonished. The parson felt that perhaps he was speaking too harshly, and yet he could only continue on. "It was *not* God who sent the enchantress. She was *not* an angel, but only a sinful human being like the rest of us. If she had the power to charm a house to clean itself and cook for itself, why could she not welcome all the beggars in the land into it? She used her power

vengefully, cruelly, as selfishly as any rank
capitalist, to punish someone who made her angry
rather than to help anyone."

Here the parson ran out of words, of breath, and
instead stabbed his ebony stick in the ground to
underline his words. It punctured a hole in the soft
green turf, and a flower grew up out of it: not a rose,
but a soft blue flower, which unfurled with open
petals like a lily – although the parson had never
seen a lily of pure blue before.

They both gazed down at it, thunderstruck. It
took some minutes to grow, and open. The parson
did not dare to look at Briarley.

But when at last the flower had opened, the
parson did look at Briarley, and his heart gave on
great queer thump and then lay like a lead weight in
his chest, for the man seemed as dragonish as ever.

"That has never happened before," Briarley said,
and his voice sounded unsteady again.

"Do you think I angered the enchantress?"

Briarley knelt by the lily. Daisy poked her head
out of his coat to sniff the petals, and sneezed; and
Briarley touched the flower, taking care to touch the
petals with the soft pads of his fingers rather than
his tearing claws. "It's soft," he said; and then to the
parson's great surprise, Briarley plucked the flower,
and thrust it at the parson, rather in the manner of a
schoolboy thrusting a flower at a girl. "Do take it."

The parson took the flower. It had a sweet clean
smell, like the scent the parson's wife Emily used to
wear, and the parson felt a moment of sadness so
intense that tears came into his eyes.

He tucked the blue lily carefully in his

buttonhole, and then raised his eyes to find Briarley gazing at him with a line of worry between his brown human eyes. The parson smiled and offered his arm, so they might walk arm in arm together, as young men had done at Oxford in the parson's day.

They did not leave behind the stem of the blue flower, but walked around the perimeter of that circle of rose hedges. Perhaps the dragon was as curious as the parson to see if it bloomed again.

But it did not. At length, the parson said, "Please forgive my outburst. My emotions carried me away, I am afraid. I have always found injustice – I have always been enraged by injustice."

"Then you do think it was unjust?" Briarley asked, with the urgency of a man begging for a sip of water in the desert.

"Yes. Very much so," the parson said; and Briarley heaved out a great sigh, and said no more. "Does that comfort you?" the parson asked, for he had the idea that it had, and yet he did not understand it.

Briarley nodded. "Yes," he said, speaking slowly, as if he did not understand either. "Mrs. Price has always said it was just punishment for our sins, and yet I have always thought it was unjust."

They took another turn around the circle. The blue lily did not blossom again.

"And yet you are right," Briarley mused. "Just because it is a sin we all commit – that does not mean it is not a sin. I had so much. I could have given her a bun and sixpence."

"It is easier to condemn sins that only other people commit," the parson said. "I think that is why the church speaks so harshly against adultery, and divorce, and homosexuality. But it was the universal sins of greed, and gluttony, and pride – the sins we rarely preach about these days – that caused the last war, and the last war planted the seeds for this."

Perhaps in these last days the enchantment was growing thin. The war, which had seemed so far away that it might almost have been in a history book, seemed very near to the parson again. It came to him with a little shock that he did not know how the tide of battle went.

"I have been thinking," Briarley said. His voice was abrupt again. "If the house does not sink into Hell, or fall into ruin. It will be empty after All Hallow's Eve. I have been thinking…" He swallowed, and the parson stood close enough that he could see the dragon's throat bob. "I must write a new will. I will leave the house for a convalescent home for wounded soldiers. Will you witness it for me?"

"Of course," the parson said. His throat swelled so much that he could not speak further, but only squeezed the dragon's arm, and hoped that told his emotion. "Of course."

***

The parson took the will into the village the next morning to send it express to Briarley's solicitors in London – which was the same firm that the Briarley Estate had used since Briarley's younger days, although the personnel of course had changed, and the parson thought of the parable of the ship, which had all its timbers replaced over the course of its voyage. The newspapers in the shop told of RAF raids in Berlin.

As he rode his bicycle back to the estate, he entertained some hope that he might find the roses wilting, and the grass growing dull with the autumn, and the curse broken altogether by this act of generosity.

But the dragon met him nearly at the gates, his nostrils smoking with impatience. The parson hid his disappointment behind a smile, and they went inside for luncheon.

But afterwards the parson escaped to his room for a few minutes, and cried, because it seemed that the last best hope was gone, and when the curse ended the dragon must die.

CHAPTER 17

Briarley Estate had no air raid sirens. The first sign the parson had of the bombing was the enormous crash and the wild sensation of being thrown out of bed.

He was on his feet again before he was fully awake, swearing in words that would have shocked dear Miss Clarence, because for some few moments he thought he was back in the trenches. Indeed, he was already buttoning his trousers when he came fully to his senses, and realized what must have happened, and knew that he must get out.

He grabbed his overcoat from its chair, and put it on as he went to check his door.

The door was cool to the touch, and the corridor dark and silent. The bomb had not struck this part of the house, it seemed, if it had struck the house at all. Perhaps it was only close.

He hurried down the corridor. "Briarley!" he shouted, and remembered in that moment that Briarley slept in his tower-top lair – directly in the path of any bombs –

"Damn it!" the parson yelled. Why had he not told the man to move to lower rooms?

But it had seemed impossible that the war should ever come here.

Another jangling crash. The sconces rattled, and the floor danced beneath the parson's feet. But this one was less violent, he thought, and came from farther away: the bombers must be moving onward, chased away from London by the gallant RAF. They were dropping the last of their payloads so they could flee faster.

The smell of smoke reached him near the end of the corridor. He had gained the stairs now, and they too were chill and dark.

"Briarley!" he shouted. His voice echoed up the staircase. "Annie! Hugh! Mrs. Price!"

He received no answer. Where did the servants sleep? Up beneath the rooftop? Down in the cellar?

He would do them no good blundering blindly about the house. They might not know of bombings, but houses had caught fire in 1840 as surely as anytime else; they would know they must get out.

The parson gained the Great Hall. Here at last he saw smoke, eddying up near the ceiling, rising from God knows where.

He strode across the tiles. He had nearly gained the door when he heard Daisy yapping.

He stopped, stricken. The dog barked and barked.

Daisy had no legs. She could not run from the flames.

"Briarley!" the parson shouted. "Do you have

her?"

But there was no answer still, no one within call; and the dog had begun to intersperse her barks with high-pitched whimpers.

She could not be so far away if he could hear that. The parson turned from the door, and cursed himself, and headed into the house to find her.

The smoke grew thicker as he went. It was not yet choking, and he hoped it would not grow so: that the dog was near the edge of the flames, and he could tuck her under his arm and carry her out, and no harm done.

The air grew hot, and hotter. His skin ached with the heat of it. Daisy's yelps grew louder, more desperate, closer he hoped – and he rounded the corner, and he had reached the dining room, and through the other door he could see a wall of fire.

But the room itself was not yet ablaze. It looked indeed some obscene parody of its changeless self: the table laid as usual with the suckling pig and the roast beef, the tablecloth burning because the candlesticks had fallen over and the linen had caught. The apples had fallen from their tower, and scattered across the floor. The parson stepped on one and fell painfully to one knee.

It was from that vantage that he saw Daisy shivering in the corner, her bright eyes reflecting the fire.

They had made a little bed for her, a basket with a soft wool blanket, and her roller skate tucked up beside. She was scrabbling at the skate with her front paws, as if she knew that it could save her, if only she could haul herself in it. The parson crawled toward her (it was easier to breathe down near the floor) and caught her up in his arms, and stuffed the roller skate in his overcoat pocket; and staggered to his feet to carry her out the door.

There was an ominous creak. The parson lifted his head – everything seemed to be moving slowly now, as it does in a moment of ultimate horror – and saw the fiery ring of the chandelier overhead, burning not only with its usual candles, but glowing itself with the horrible brightness of hot metal.

The chandelier tore loose from the ceiling, and swung down against the wall. And then the ceiling fell after it, and a vast burning beam fell right across the door.

The parson's mind became very calm in moments of crisis. This had held him in good stead in the last war, and it meant, now, that he surveyed their options with a clear calm eye. The room had no windows. Fire blocked both the doors. There was no way out.

He was going to burn to death – or rather suffocate, and be burned after – and Rose would never know what had happened to him. Even if she came here – and she would come here, once the letters stopped – she would not know what happened: for the house would still stand, and the roses still bloom, as if the bombs had never been…

He took a step toward the door. But the burning heat of the fire was like a physical wall, and he could no more step through it than he could step through stone; and he retreated, instead, struggling to hold Daisy, who thrashed frantically in his arms.

He crouched down low. Heat and smoke both

rise, and the air down low was still comparatively breathable, although still bad enough to make his eyes sting. His skin felt stretched and tight. "It's all right, it's all right," he told the dog, and kissed her soft head. "At least we shall not die alone – I was always afraid to die alone."

It did not calm the dog at all. Her tail whipped back and forth in terror, her little paws scrabbled at his arm, and she barked and barked and barked.

If Rose came before the curse ended – if she could get leave again – surely Annie would tell her what had happened. Had Annie gotten out? Had anyone gotten out? Would the curse end, if they all burned?

There was a great crash somewhere not too far away. The parson held Daisy close, so close that he could feel her frantic heartbeat and still more frantic barking – felt more than heard it, because the roar of the flame seemed to block all other sound. Would it be the kind thing to break her neck now, before the fire got them?

The thought seemed to take a terrible material shape as he had it. A great black Satanic silhouette loomed in the blocked doorway, its wings spread, its back straining; and then the fallen rafter rose, and was cast aside, and Briarley's voice rose above the war of the flames. "Edward!"

"Briars!" the parson shouted, and he was on his feet and stumbling toward the voice, although his legs slithered like noodles beneath him, and his smoke-sodden head swam. But he did not need to run any farther: Briarley ran to him, and enveloped him in a wet towel, and was carrying him out of the room.

"I have Daisy," the parson was saying, and Daisy was barking, and the parson was repeating, "I have Daisy, I have Daisy – "

And Briars was saying, his voice rough from the smoke, "You should not have gone after her – you should have let me get her. You should have let me get her, you stupid man, I am immune to fire."

***

This was not, it turned out, strictly true. Briarley carried them outside, the little dog and the parson, and all but dropped them on the lawn to beat out the embers speckling his own clothes, and it was then that the parson saw the blisters speckling his hands.

"My good man!" he cried. "Your hands – let me see."

Briarley held out his hands, obedient, and the parson could see the ugly burns striped across his palms, from where he had lifted that rafter. He did not think – he was smoke-addled beyond thinking – he took Briarley's hands in both of his and kissed them, and Briarley snatched them away again and hid them behind his back. "It was nothing," he insisted.

"Nothing!" the parson cried. "You saved our lives!"

"I should not have had to do any such thing if you were not a fool," the dragon said. The words might have sounded angry, but he wrapped an arm around the parson's shoulder and the parson pounded him on the back, and they were both laughing with relief.

Daisy whined at their feet. The dragon dropped down beside her, and reached for her, and flinched back when she nosed at his blistered hand. The parson knelt, his knees creaking, and pulled the shivering dog on his lap.

That was when the servants arrived. Annie yelled, "Thank God, they're alive!"

And she cast a bucket of water over the parson. It was a relief after that flame and scorching heat.

The parson turned toward her, and realized with a shock that he could – *almost* see her: the air was so thick with ash that her invisibility cleared a space within it.

Behind her, too, came two other clear shapes in the sooty night: one tall, and one small and light, and both carrying buckets; and then Annie was crying, "Daisy!" An almost-visible hand ruffled the dog's ears, and Daisy tried to lick it.

"Lord be praised," Mrs. Price said. And she knelt down by the parson, her bucket clinking on the ground, and she lifted water in her cupped hands – so that the semicircle of it seemed to hover in the air – and held it out for the dog to drink.

There came a great creak from the house. Another rafter fell in, and sparks flew up. "Do you think the magic will be after fixing this, now?" Annie asked.

"I s'pose we could live in the cellars till the curse gives out," Hugh replied soberly.

The parson turned to ask Briarley his opinion. But Briarley no longer stood there: he had moved a few yards off, his wings half open and his head

144

tilted up to the sky.

The parson felt a sudden intense foreboding. "Briarley!" he called. But his smoke-seared voice did not carry very far, and Briarley didn't hear; so the parson went over to him. "Briars! Come along with us, then. There must be somewhere that we can shelter for the night."

Briarley did not turn away from the sky. The hot wind blowing off the house ruffled his neck frill.

Daisy wriggled in the parson's arms, and let loose a little bark. "Briars," the parson said.

"Lead the servants down to the old caretaker's cottage," Briarley said. "I'm going after them."

"After – the *planes*?" the parson said, incredulous. "Briars, they're miles from here by now. You'll never catch up!"

"Don't tell me what to do!" Briarley flared. Fire billowed from his nostrils.

"The bombers all have gunners," the parson persisted. "Even if you did catch them, they'd shoot you down out of the sky!"

"They bombed my house," Briarley replied. His voice had taken on a deadly calm more horrible than any outward rage. "They nearly killed you. And they shall pay."

"And what if you get one of our planes by mistake?" He tried to grab Briarley's arm, as if he had the strength to hold him back.

Briarley shook him off. The whites of his eyes gleamed red in the reflected firelight. "Unhand me!"

Daisy began to bark. "Don't do it, man!" the parson shouted.

But the dragon – for he seemed all dragon now,

as he had on the first night that the parson knew him – lifted off with a powerful thrust of his wings, and flashed upward into the sky. For a few moments, the parson could see him in the fiery light of the house, soaring after the retreating planes; and then he disappeared into the darkness.

***

The parson hardly knew what happened next. He thrust Daisy into Annie's arms and hurried after Briarley, as if he might make any kind of time following him cross-country, and on foot.

The rose hedges, usually a twisted labyrinth, parted before him like the Red Sea. He had a straight shot down to a little door in the wall behind the house, and he went out through it.

The moon glowed silver and calm on the countryside beyond. Its light outlined the retreating planes, so their stiff straight wings looked like dark cutouts in the silver sky. Briarley flew behind them, his broad bat wings spread wide as he soared after the enemy planes. A sudden furious stream of flame burst out of him.

He was too far away to see clearly. Yet the parson seemed to see him in agonizing detail.

Bright flashes bloomed out of the planes, so far away that they were silent, and pretty, like fireworks. But that was gunfire.

"Briarley!" the parson shouted. "Briarley! *Briars!*"

It was as if his words were a bullet. Almost at that moment, something knocked Briarley off his course, and he tumbled out of the sky. He turned over and over, too far away from the parson to see with any clearness, and yet he seemed to see everything, until the black shape merged with the blackness of the land below.

"Briarley!" the parson screamed, as if the young man were not hopelessly beyond call. And then he began to run.

An old overgrown track led away from the house. The parson followed it, running faster than he had run since he had charged on the Somme. This time he had no gun, no pack, no fear to hold him back, and he ran as if by running he might reach Briarley, in all the vastness of the moonlit English countryside.

The parson had no breath to shout. His throat, already scoured by the smoke, ached with every breath, and he tasted blood at the back of his mouth. But he ran on, his eyes fixed on that spot where Briarley had vanished into the darkness.

He could not be dead. He could not be dead. The thought beat in the parson's head with every rasping breath. Briarley could not be dead, when he had just risked his own life to save the parson and sweet Daisy, when at last perhaps he was just beginning to learn how to love, and when the parson was learning –

The parson tripped. Indeed it was a miracle that he had not tripped before, running pell-mell in the darkness. But now his luck caught up with him, and he fell hard over a root and went sprawling.

He lay on the ground, gasping for breath. He began to cough, and for a time he felt as though he might suffocate there on the ground, drowning in thin air.

But at last he got his breath. He spit out a glob of phlegm, and dragged himself back up to his knees, and looked out across that quiet silvery countryside.

And it was then that reality struck him, like a blow across the face. Briarley had fallen: he was lost somewhere far away in the darkness, and the parson would not find him. He let out a sound, not loud, a gasping moan, and curled in on himself. "Damn you, Briarley," he gasped, and then began to sob.

He held his breath to hold the sobs back: it was a trick he had learned as a child. But at his next breath, another sob burst out, and the force of it bent him nearly double. His face pressed against the cold scratchy grass. He smacked his hand against the earth, repeatedly, and kicked the ground, and curled up on his side on the ground like a beaten dog, and still could not stop the tears from flowing.

The fire had parched him. He ran out of tears before he ran out of sobs. For a while he lay on the ground, dry-eyed, his face crushed against the scratchy sleeve of his overcoat, each sob jerking through his body as if he had been given an electrical shock.

But at last – at last – the sobs subsided too. The parson lay quiet on the cold ground, cold and stiff all over, until the thought came to him quite suddenly that if he did not get up, he was going to die there.

And he had to live, he remembered. He had forgotten for a little while. But he had to live, for

Rose.

He lifted his face from his arm, and blinked at finding the world still silver in the moonlight. One felt it ought to go dark – that there ought to be thunder and lightning, as there had been the evening he had received word of Rupert's death.

But Emily had died on a beautiful spring morning, just after the daffodils bloomed.

The parson staggered to his feet. They were bare – he had forgotten till now – bare and cold, and battered from the run across the countryside. His bad leg ached with cold and overuse.

Behind him, the Briarley Estate still blazed. The parson stared at it until he could no longer hold up his heavy head. Then his head drooped forward, his body bent like an old man's, and he began the long trudge back to the broken house.

CHAPTER 18

It was just barely dawn when the parson reached the wall of the estate. The fire was out now, leaving behind only a haze of smoke that caught the pink glow of dawn; and that was very beautiful, and the parson, who was nearly numb with cold and pain, was caught for a moment by the loveliness, and it made him want to cry.

But his eyes were too dry for tears, and he dropped back into numbness again. There was a little door in the wall, he saw, a tradesman's door probably. The knob turned easily under his numb cold hand, and he walked into the Briarley grounds.

He stopped a moment in the doorway, still holding the knob, to gaze at the house. One half of it was nothing but smoking rubble. The other half still stood, and he wondered if there was anything left in the house, or if it was only an empty burnt-out hull.

But then he let go of the door and it swung shut and his head drooped down, so that he only saw the frost-rimed grass. His heavy legs could barely lift his leaden feet above the cold hard ground.

"Mr. Harper! Mr. Harper! Oh, Mr. Harper, you're alive! Oh, that's all we needed to make this the happiest day on earth!"

A tall Amazon of a girl was running down the path toward him, her face and her dress smudged with soot. He stared at her, blinking, not understanding, until she had nearly reached him, and then she cried, "Mr. Harper! Is Mr. Briarley with you?"

"Annie!" he cried, and it was only as he heard himself say her name that he understood who she was, and what must have happened, and then his strength gave out and he sat right down on the cold frosted grass.

The curse was broken. Perhaps it had broken when Briarley died.

"Mr. Harper?" Annie said.

Somewhere above the parson's head, Daisy began to bark.

The parson lifted his head. Mrs. Price had arrived too, with Daisy in her thin arms. The dog wriggled and barked, batting at the air with her short front legs as if she wanted to catapult herself into the parson's lap.

Mrs. Price pressed a quelling hand on top of Daisy's head, and the dog stilled. "God bless us all," she said, and knelt down in the grass beside him, comprehension in her eyes.

Annie looked between the two of them, her joyful face disintegrating into concern. "What is it?" she asked, and her voice grew urgent, almost defiant. "What is it, then?" she demanded. "He broke the curse! We're all right now! Where is Mr. Briarley?"

"Greater love," the parson said, and his voice broke and his head fell forward as if all strength had gone out of his neck. "Greater love hath no man than this, that a man lay down his life for his friends…"

Annie gazed at him, uncomprehending. Then her face crumpled. "It *can't* be!" she cried, and she burst into sobs, and cast herself on her knees and buried her face in Mrs. Price's lap. Daisy licked her ear.

Mrs. Price patted her hair. "There, there, child," she said. "We've all lived long past our time anyhow."

"But we haven't got to live at all!" Annie cried. "We've been trapped here in the roses for years and years, and at last he's saved us, and he doesn't get to share it!"

The parson could not bear it. He stood up, although his bad leg nearly gave out beneath him. But he held his breath and held himself up, and limped away, although each step felt as if someone had thrust a knife right up through his foot and sliced along his shinbone. Like the Little Mermaid… Rose had hated that story… the Little Mermaid who gave up her voice for feet, although each step she took felt like she was walking on knives. "And all for a human man, when there must be perfectly nice mermen," Rose had said…

The parson veered off the path without meaning to: his tottering steps had put him astray. He walked into a rosebush, and snatched at the thorny branches to hold himself upright; and the parson noticed, only then, that the roses had all died. The black shriveled blossoms still clung to the bushes, their petals like witch's fingers.

"Is this what you wanted?" he asked the rosebush, as if those dead flowers were indeed the hands of that long-ago enchantress. But a chilly wind blew up, and the dead flowers rattled, and fell apart in flakes as the parson disentangled himself from the bush.

He staggered on toward the front of the house. The front steps were unharmed. They led up to a burnt-out door, and through the empty arch of the doorway the parson could see the lightening sky.

A young man sat on those steps, his arms around his legs and his head against his knees. "Hugh?" the parson said.

The young man lifted his head, and the parson saw his red-rimmed eyes and his great red-tipped beak of a nose. "I heard you tell the others," he said. "I came up here so…"

The parson sat heavily beside him, and put a hand on his shoulder. He hoped that the hand offered some warmth and comfort, because his heart was a stone in his body and he did not think he could offer it in any other way.

"Did it break because he died?" Hugh asked. "Would it have broken long ago, if we'd killed him?"

The parson's hand clouted Hugh's head so sharply that it knocked Hugh off the steps. "Go away!" the parson shouted. "Go on! How dare you say that?"

Hugh turned around, his chest heaving, fists clenched. He was a tall well-built young man, and he might have beaten the parson to a pulp.

The parson made no attempt to get away. He sat where he was, on the front steps of Briarley Hall, with his back straight and his chin lifted so that he looked as fierce and proud as the prow of a ship. Hugh shook out his fists, like a man trying to shake his hands dry, and walked swiftly away, around to the back of the house.

The parson sat. Even sitting he could feel the pain shooting up through his legs. His bare feet looked very white in the pearly dawn light, and he wondered if they might be freezing, and if he would lose a toe. But it all seemed very far from him, and he did not particularly care.

He sat for some time in that flat gray haze of exhaustion and grief. Petals of soot swirled on the wind. The parson took one in the eye, and his eye blinked and watered with the attempt to wash it out.

The sound of wheels on gravel did not rouse him till it was very close indeed. He lifted his head at the sound of weak brakes squealing to a halt, and he saw that the iron gates were open, and the white raked drive speckled black with soot, and a lorry had driven up almost to the foot of the stairs.

The spell had been broken indeed: and the modern world had come to Briarley Hall.

CHAPTER 19

The parson walked slowly down the steps to the lorry. He felt very old and stiff as he went, as if he had aged a decade in one night, and wondered fleetingly if his hair had turned white.

A stout gray-haired man in a Civil Defence cap swung out of the truck. He had a red face and sensible tweeds and the general look of a retired military man, and he spoke with a gruffness so true to form that the parson found it reassuring.

"I'm Colonel Haverford," the man said. "Is this Briarley Hall?"

"Yes," the parson said.

"Funny, that," Colonel Haverford mused. He gazed up at the hall with a baffled expression on his round face. "I've lived near Briarfield since I retired on half pay ten years ago, but I've never heard of this place."

The parson was mustering his scattered mental forces to tell the story of the reclusive owner, who did not go out in society, etc. – but then Colonel

Haverford turned to him, and answered his own not-quite-asked question, when he said, "We found a man who claims he owns the place. Mad as a hare, *I* think."

The parson's head swooped. He had to grab to bonnet of the lorry to hold himself upright.

"Steady on now!" Colonel Haverford said. "Seems quite harmless, if you ask me, even if he *is* cracked. Of course he might be a kraut spy, but if he is, well, we've got him now, haven't we?"

"No, no," the parson said. "It's not that. It's just that the young master – " A burble of helpless laughter rose to his lips, joy effervescing out of him even as he reminded himself that it might not, indeed *could not be* Briarley, for surely Colonel Haverford would have noticed such protuberances as wings. "He *does* come across a bit cracked. We thought he was dead."

"Well, now," Colonel Haverford said. "Easy enough to check. I've got him in the back seat, see…"

But his voice trailed off. He was looking over the grounds now, and had caught sight of Annie and Mrs. Price, in their long old-fashioned dresses with the leg-of-mutton sleeves. "I say," he said, affronted. "Were you having some sort of fancy dress ball last night? There's a war on, you know."

"It's old clothes from the attics," the parson said, almost feverish with impatience. "Mr. Briarley has got this delusion that it is the 1840s… brain fever, you know…"

"Brain fever," the colonel agreed. The explanation seemed to please him. He tugged his mustache, and nodded comprehendingly. "Rum thing, isn't it? Well, I've other business to attend to this morning, and no doubt you can look after him better than I can."

"Doubtless," the parson said, so impatient that he could have kicked the man.

But Colonel Haverford was already throwing open the back door. The parson limped after him – God, what he would have given for that ivory-handled stick! For any stick at all! – and nearly howled in disappointment at the sight of the young man lying on the back seat.

A young man. A young man with golden hair, and not a dragon at all.

Well, naturally Colonel Haverford would have mentioned it if he had found a winged man. What did the parson expect? But he felt sick and empty with disappointment.

"I say!" Colonel Haverford was yelling. His voice seemed very distant now. "You lot! Step back!"

The young man twisted round. He had ludicrous fluffy sideburns, and...

Brown eyes. The parson knew those eyes.

"Briars," the parson blurted. He leaned into the lorry, and grasped the young man's hand, and kissed him on the mouth.

***

It was some time before the parson's heart stopped thundering.

No one knew; no one had seen. The lorry door

had hidden them from view, and in any case Colonel Haverford had been busy shooing away Annie and Hugh and Mrs. Price from the lorry, which they had been exploring with the brazen curiosity of children. They had forgotten they were visible, perhaps; and they disconcerted Colonel Haverford by their positive delight in the fact.

"Rum lot," Colonel Haverford confided to the parson. "I don't suppose they've all caught brain fever too?"

"I imagine the bombing left them just a bit hysterical," the parson said, trying to sound grave, although his heart was pounding in his ears so loudly that he could scarcely hear Colonel Haverford's words.

He drove off. And then there were tears and handshakes as the servants came to greet Mr. Briarley, "back from the dead," as Mrs. Price put it, "risen up again like Lazarus when Our Lord put his hand on him – "

She threw her apron over her head to hide her tears.

Hugh shook Mr. Briarley's hand, looking mortified and bashful, and Annie took his hands in both of hers and kissed them.

But the reunion passed, and they scattered. Annie and Hugh headed to Briarfield – "To Briarfield!" Annie shouting, leaping in the air as she ran, like a schoolgirl released on holiday – and Mrs. Price bustled back into the still-standing half of the hall, to see what could be salvaged of the kitchen.

The parson remained seated on the grass. It was dry and dull, as autumn grass should be, and he occupied himself in picking stems. He attempted to honk one, as he had known how to do as a boy, but either he had lost the trick or the October grass was too brittle.

Briarley sat down beside him. The parson did not look at him at first, but he could feel his presence there, the heat and the weight of him. At last he risked a glance, and discovered the man gazing in wonder at himself: his own bare hands, with regular fingernails in the place of his old curved claws, and his own bare feet red with the cold. There were slashes sewn into the back of his shirt – for his wings – and through them the parson could see his pale back, the surprising vulnerable slenderness of his shoulder blades.

Briarley lifted a trembling hand to his own face, feeling the silly sideburns on his cheeks, the bridge of his nose, the faint growth of stubble on his chin. The parson's lips still tingled from the burn of it.

"He did not flinch from me," Briarley said, and looked at the parson, as if he needed confirmation before he could trust the evidence of his own eyes and hands.

"My dear Briars," said the parson, "Of course he saw nothing odd."

Briarley gazed down at his hands again. He touched the pads of his thumbs to each fingernail. "The curse is broken?"

"It very much seems that way," the parson said.

"And all I needed to do all this time was run into a burning building?" Briarley sounded indignant.

"That is not such a small thing," the parson said gently.

They sat for some time side by side. Briarley gazed in wonder at his hands, and the parson grew more uncomfortable by the moment. It seemed that they would not speak of that kiss, and it was probably just as well, but all the same he seemed to feel it hanging above his head like the sword of Damocles.

"You look quite different too," Briarley said, his words breaking in on the parson's thoughts.

The parson shifted. "I have always been an old man," he said. "As long as you have known me."

"You are not so old as all that," Briarley said. "And anyway, I am 120."

The parson looked at him – sitting there in the flower of his youth, with red lips and red cheeks and the wind fingering his golden hair – and began to laugh.

"Well I am!" Briarley insisted. "I shall turn 121 on All Hallow's Eve. But that is not what I meant. My eyes are seeing differently now. Before, as a dragon – it is hard to explain; I saw heat – indeed I do not know how to explain it, to someone who has never seen it. It is a different color and one we have no word for. But now I see color again, as I used to do." And then he reached over and poked the parson's cheek playfully. "Your cheeks are red," he said; and he tugged an errant lock of the parson's hair, grown long, for the parson had not had a haircut since he came to the estate. "And your hair – would you call that chestnut? Certainly it is not gray."

The parson was too tired for games. It seemed to him that Briarley was teasing him, and it was unkind. He pushed the man's hand away, and said, with a briskness he did not feel, "We had better decide what to do, now that you have all rejoined the world again. We shall have to look over the house and see if any of it is salvageable. It looks as it a good half of it might be all right, and that could go some way for the war effort – "

He pushed himself to stand, but pain lanced through his legs, and the parson crashed down again like a sack of potatoes. The world swam for a moment, and when it cleared again he found Briarley gazing into his face, wide-eyed, angry. "You're getting ready to leave," he accused. "You want to get everything in order and then just go."

"I'm not going anywhere just yet," the parson snapped. He was not indeed quite certain that he could walk back to the house, let alone ride his bicycle anywhere. If his bicycle had survived the bombing.

"The curse is broken, your work is done, and you're ready to wash your hands of me," Briarley said. "And you kissed me!" he cried, accusing.

The parson winced, and blushed red as a schoolboy, and tugged at an obstinate strand of grass. "I had thought you were dead," he offered, in explanation.

"And were you glad I was alive?" Briarley demanded.

"Yes!" the parson shouted. "Yes, I was glad you were alive! I would have missed you sorely, you stupid man!"

Briarley looked flummoxed. He rubbed his hand over his chin – how strange that he had a chin! How strange that he had a mouth, and lips, which bunched together in perplexity! "Then why are you in a hurry to leave?"

"Oh," said the parson. A wash of tiredness rushed over him. He felt that he might cry from sheer exhaustion. "There's a war on, Briars. You may have noticed last night. I have duties to my parish, which I have been neglecting, and you shall have duties here – or in the army. I imagine you would make a good pilot for the RAF. Certainly you have logged more flight hours than most of the boys they send up." And he began to laugh again, mirthlessly, because he knew how short a pilot's life could be, and it seemed unfair – unfair – unfair – to have brought Briarley through the curse, only to send him off to die. But then it was no more unfair than the sacrifice expected of every other pilot, was it, who had not had 120 years?

"Couldn't we," Briarley said, and stopped, and began again. "Couldn't we," he said – and couldn't finish his sentence – and instead, took the parson's face in both his hands, very gently, and kissed him just as gently on the mouth.

It was a far longer and more thorough kiss than the parson had given him earlier, and they were both trembling when Briarley drew back. He released the parson's face reluctantly, and let his hands fall on the parson's shoulders, and pushed him back against the grass and crawled over him, so that they were kissing again, and the parson's hands were in Briarley's soft hair.

"Briars," he murmured. "Briars. Briars – "

He said the name in between kisses, until

Briarley drew back, and looked him in the face. "Edward?" he said, and the parson pushed him off, so they were sitting side by side again, and perfectly respectable if anyone happened to come up the lane – so long as no one looked closely, and saw that they were holding hands.

"It is only – " said Briarley, and lifted the parson's hand and began to kiss the knuckles. "Even if you can't stay here – even if I have to join the army – I can understand if you *want* to go – when you never wanted to be here – "

"Come now," the parson said. "I had opportunity enough to go."

"But your sense of duty made you stay. I know it. That's over and done with now. If God sent you here, you have accomplished what He wanted of you. But if you – if you don't want to leave – if it is just that you *have* to go…"

Here he seemed to lose his words, and instead just lowered his head over the parson's hand, his lips against the parson's palm, his long golden eyelashes low over his eyes.

"We both have our duty," the parson said. "We will be split up – perhaps for the duration. But that does not mean – does it? – that everything has to be over between us. The war cannot last forever. I cannot think a few more years will be so terrible, when you have already waited for a hundred."

Briarley let out a choked cracked sound, and pulled the parson into a hug. The parson put his arms around him, and rested his weary head against Briarley's shoulder, and let Briarley cling to him until at last the man let go.

They were perhaps both a little watery-eyed after that. The parson reached for a handkerchief, realized that of course he had not taken time to grab one with the roof falling down about his head, and simply smiled through his tears instead.

"In any case," the parson said, "I will not be leaving just yet. I will need some time to recover before I can go anywhere. Indeed," he admitted, though it pained him, "I do not think I can walk at all just now."

"What?" Concern colored Briarley's face. "Were you injured in the bombing?"

"I was injured in running after you, you foolish man," the parson said. "I saw you fall out of the sky."

"Did you!"

"It was like watching the fall of Icarus," the parson said, his voice flat with suppressed emotion.

"Was it?" And now Briarley's voice was soft.

"And I ran after you," the parson said, "and tried to find you, and could not."

He was too English to tell the rest of it: that he had fallen to his knees in a dark place, and cried as though his heart would break. He said only, "It was a long walk back."

But perhaps Briarley understood what he did not say, because he was gazing at the parson with a softness in his eyes. And then he smiled: and with a smile on his lips, his face was the face of an angel.

"Well," said Briarley. "I shall see to it that you do not have to walk at all till it is well."

And he gathered the parson up in his arms – not quite so effortlessly as he had in his dragon days.

But still he made no complaint as he carried the parson up the gravel drive to the still smoking ruins of the house. He went around to the side of the house that still stood, and found a small closed door: and the door swung open quietly at his touch, and he carried the parson over the threshold.

Made in the USA
Columbia, SC
27 November 2023

27204470R00105